Value of Blood

The Price of Truth

by

ARTEMIS CRAIG

Front Cover image by Rebecacovers

Inspired by Anjie Williams Brown

Edited by Roe Braddy

ISBN:978-0-9890876-3-6

Published by Artemis Craig Publishing Gardendale, AL

www.artemiscraigbooks.com

DEDICATION

This is dedicated to Cyreatha Nichelle Craig-Radcliff aka "Nikki" in honor of our sisterhood. I was blessed to have you love me and walk beside me on my journey.

SYNOPSIS

Simetra Thomas, an office manager at a hospital, befriends Spencer Walach and helps him access the mental health services he desperately needs. However, during a treatment session, Spencer suffers a fatal electrocution, leaving Simetra feeling guilty and determined to uncover the truth behind his tragic accident.

As Simetra investigates, she faces a devastating blow when her brother Nevell Carter ends up in a coma from a car accident, forcing her to assume the role of his guardian and conservator. Meanwhile, Detective Levi Stone encounters resistance from the hospital's administration while probing into Spencer's death. His investigation reveals that key witnesses are mysteriously turning up dead.

As Nevell dies under suspicious circumstances, Simetra finds herself wrongfully accused of his murder, becoming a fugitive. Devona Drummond, the hospital administrator's assistant, antagonizes Simetra, and her qualities of rivalry and deception complicate Simetra's efforts to clear her name. In Simetra's quest to prove her innocence, she uncovers a sinister network of organized crime. She struggles to evade a relentless killer determined to silence her before she can expose the truth.

"The Value of Blood: The Price of Truth" delves into the themes of guilt, justice, and the lengths one will go to protect their loved ones. Simetra's journey illustrates the struggle against systemic failures of institutions meant to provide support, while highlighting the moral complexities in a world where powerful entities often obscure the truth.

Value of Blood: The Price of Truth is an outstanding thriller. If you love smart twists, and turns, you will thoroughly enjoy this book. It is emotionally grounded storytelling *that will keep you glued to every word.* Artemis Craig proves that she is a master of thriller novels.

Anjetta (Anjie) Williams-Brown

Artemis Craig's writing is fire. Her newest release, "Value of Blood" will leave you sitting on the edge of your seat, biting your nails and praying for the FMC. The lady has edge. She's sharp, so watch out for all the surprises you will find in each chapter. I have only one piece of advice. READ VOB NOW!

Roe Braddy

Acknowledgements:

Special thanks to my son, Roderic Jernigan Jr., for believing in me. To my grandson, Gregrory, who loves Nahnee unconditionally.

Thank you to those who encouraged me to stay true to myself, especially my sister-cousin Anjie, my sister Chyrel, and my best friend Karen, who kept me on task.

Thank you to my sister Cheryl, who reminds me to take care of my health. A special thanks to Rawle I AM James, who heard my voice and challenged me to reclaim it. Rest in Heaven, "King." I miss you every day.

"It's not what you think about me, it's what I think about you that counts." By Clifford Craig, Sr. (My Father)

Value of Blood

Darkness holds many secrets,

The truth shall come to light,

As sure as the day emerges from night.

Danger hides in the shadows,

Death lurks behind every door,

The consequence of what you have in store.

The truth is ever elusive, yet beckons you to come near,

You accept the challenge, placing justice over fear.

At a hefty price comes accountability,

Your life may be required of you as a possibility.

To what lengths are you willing to go to justify

Kinship and the value of blood

Search your soul, this journey is not for the weak,

Be prepared for the unexpected as you uncover the

Answers you seek.

Artemis Craig

CHAPTER 1

The warehouse stretched endlessly; its towering shelves were crammed with neatly organized medical supplies. The sterile glow of overhead lights bounced off the metal surfaces, casting long, stark shadows that danced eerily across the floor.

In the center of the space, robotic forklifts moved with mechanical precision. Each machine expertly lifted pallets stacked high with equipment and supplies, maneuvering them onto a platform that looked like a modernized dumbwaiter. With a hum of machinery, the platform ascended smoothly toward the ceiling, where a set of articulated robotic arms awaited. The arms reached out, their movements fluid yet calculated, as they transferred the products onto the upper shelves with ease.

Amidst the hum of robotics and the faint clatter of machinery, the distinct echo of footsteps punctuated the air. The sound grew louder, purposeful, drawing the focus down a narrow aisle lined with rows of prosthetic limbs. Metallic arms and legs gleamed under the artificial light, their unnatural stillness lending an unsettling quality to the scene.

A pair of boots came into view, their steady tread halting before a massive steel kennel. Inside, a hulking pit bull sat in the center, its muscular frame taut with silent energy. Its amber eyes gleamed with intelligence as it regarded the man before it. Though the dog made no sound, the tension in the air thickened, as if the animal's mere presence commanded the space.

The man stood still, his face obscured by the shadows, yet his stance betrayed neither fear nor hesitation. The pit bull didn't move, but its gaze remained fixed, a silent challenge—or perhaps, a warning.

The man's boots were just visible in the stark light spilling from above, scuffed and deliberate in their placement. His gloved hands emerged from the shadows, holding a bundle of raw, bloody steaks. Without hesitation, he tossed the meat into the kennel.

The massive pit bull didn't flinch. Its body remained as still as a marble statue, every muscle coiled and ready beneath its sleek, black coat. Only its eyes moved, locked on the shadowy figure beyond the bars. The light caught a glimmer of amber in its gaze—steady, calculating, and unnervingly intelligent.

The man took a step closer, his face still shrouded in darkness. The faint creak of leather gloves accompanied the flex of his hands, but he made no sound otherwise. The pit bull didn't break its stare, its focus unyielding despite the rich scent of fresh meat wafting through the air.

"**Hades**," the man said, his voice low and commanding, slicing through the quiet. "Devour."

The transformation was instant. With a snarl that rippled through the kennel, the dog lunged forward and sank its teeth into one of the steaks. Flesh tore with a sickening sound, and the pit bull's powerful jaws worked with brutal efficiency. The raw, primal energy of the animal was unleashed in a display of ferocity, but its eyes—those piercing amber eyes—never left the man.

The figure stood silent and motionless, watching the beast consume its offering. The faintest curl of a shadowed smile seemed to form, but the dim lighting kept his expression unreadable.

The production plant buzzed with life. Workers crowded around long, cluttered tables, their hands deftly assembling parts and devices. The hum of machinery mingled with the clatter of tools, creating a chaotic yet oddly rhythmic soundtrack to the night. Laughter and jokes punctuated the din as the workers traded quips and stories, their camaraderie evident in the ease of their movements.

In the shadows of a dimly lit corner, **Spencer Walach** stood apart from the commotion. His phone was held up, its lens trained on the bustling scene. He moved the phone slowly, capturing every detail—the workers, the parts, the machines. The faint glow of the screen illuminated his face as he paused to review the footage. Satisfied, he quickly tapped out a message, attaching the video and sending it to an unknown number.

The background noise swallowed the soft whoosh of the sent message, but another sound caught his attention—low and menacing. A growl.

Spencer froze. The sound had come from his right. He turned his head slowly, his pulse quickening.

In the gloom, a pit bull emerged, its lips curled back to reveal sharp, glistening teeth. Its growl deepened, a rumble that seemed to vibrate through the air. The dog's stance was rigid, its muscles taut beneath its sleek coat.

Beside the dog stood a man—a tall figure shrouded in mystery. A ball cap cast shadows over his face, but it was the mask that completed the unsettling image. The man stood perfectly still, his presence more intimidating than the growling dog at his side.

Spencer's breath hitched as his eyes darted between the dog and the masked man. The lively noise of the production plant seemed distant now, swallowed by the tension radiating from the darkened corner. The man's posture was calm, controlled, but there was an air of quiet menace in the way he stood—an unspoken warning.

The glow of Spencer's phone flickered in his hand, the message sent but now forgotten as he faced the silent figure and the snarling beast.

The man's voice cut through the tension like a blade. "What the hell do you think you're doing here, Walach?"

Spencer flinched at the harshness of the words, but he straightened his posture, trying to muster some courage. "I didn't want to believe it," he said, his voice trembling but resolute. "So, I came to see it for myself."

The masked man tilted his head slightly, the faintest hint of amusement in his posture. "That's unfortunate."

Spencer's eyes widened, his shock palpable. He took a step back, his resolve wavering as the implications of the man's words sunk in. "I'm not going to let you get away with this," he said, his voice rising in defiance.

The masked man chuckled softly, the sound low and menacing. "Nobody likes a tattletale." He turned his head slightly, his gaze shifting to the dog at his side. "Hades, get something in your mouth."

The dog responded instantly, springing forward with terrifying speed. Its powerful body launched toward Spencer, jaws open and teeth gleaming. Spencer had barely a moment to react before the impact sent him staggering backward.

The world tilted as Spencer fell. Behind him, a large window framed the dark night landscape, the city lights twinkling in the distance. The glass shattered on impact, the sharp sound echoing in his ears as shards sprayed outward.

Time seemed to slow as Spencer tumbled through the broken window, his body twisting in midair. Below, the drainage system caught the plant's runoff, a steady stream of water rushing toward a larger body beyond.

He hit the water hard, the cold shock ripping the air from his lungs as he was dragged into the current. Broken glass floated around him, glinting like sinister stars in the faint light. The roar of the water and the sting of the impact blurred his senses, but one thing was clear—he had to move, or he wouldn't survive.

Above, the masked man stepped closer to the shattered window. His silhouette loomed against the chaos, calm and composed as he looked down into the dark. A faint smirk tugged at the corner of his lips beneath the mask, but he didn't linger. He turned, the dog following obediently at his side, leaving the broken glass and the rushing water behind.

CHAPTER 2

The alley beside Mercy Hospital was cloaked in the dim light of a fading evening. Shadows stretched long against the brick walls, their edges softened by the amber glow of a nearby streetlamp. The faint hum of the city's rush hour buzzed in the background, muffled by the narrow space.

Spencer Walach, in his mid-fifties, lay sprawled on the cold, damp ground. His clothes were ragged, caked in grime, and his face bore the unmistakable scars of a devastating fall. His once handsome features were likened to Richard Gere. His present disfigurement gave him a haunting, almost unrecognizable appearance. He writhed in his sleep, mumbling incoherently as his body twitched with the echoes of some private torment.

His mumbling grew louder, escalating into cries as he thrashed against an invisible threat. Then, with a guttural yell, he bolted upright, his breath ragged and his eyes wide with terror. The memory of his nightmare clung to him, vivid and suffocating, as he glanced wildly around the alley.

A younger man, lean and wiry, stepped cautiously toward him. **Cecil**, another lost soul who had found refuge in the city's forgotten corners, held out his hands in a gesture of calm. "Hey, take it easy," Cecil said softly, crouching slightly as if approaching a wounded animal.

Spencer's gaze snapped to Cecil, his disoriented mind unable to process friend from foe. His body reacted before his thoughts could catch up. With a sudden burst of strength, he lunged at Cecil, his hands locking around the younger man's throat.

Cecil stumbled backward, gasping and clawing at Spencer's grip. "Wait—stop!" he choked out, his voice strained. His fingers pried desperately at Spencer's hands, his wide eyes pleading for mercy.

But Spencer was lost in the haze of panic and survival. His mind replayed fragments of the horrors he had endured—the growling dog, the masked man, the shattering glass. The alley blurred around him, the present dissolving into a warped recollection of betrayal and violence.

Cecil coughed and sputtered, his strength waning as he tried to free himself. "I'm... trying to help!" he rasped, his voice barely audible against the strain of Spencer's grip.

For a moment, Spencer froze, his grip faltering as Cecil's words pierced through the fog of his mind. Recognition flickered in his eyes, a brief clarity that began to break through the chaos. He loosened his hold, his breathing still heavy, and staggered back a step, his expression a mix of confusion and guilt.

Cecil collapsed to his knees, coughing and rubbing his throat. His long dirty dreads falling into his dirt-smattered face. "Damn, man," he wheezed, shooting Spencer a wary glance. "What the hell's wrong with you?"

Spencer ran a trembling hand over his scarred face, his body shaking with adrenaline and shame. He didn't answer. Instead, he sank back against the wall of the alley, his haunted gaze fixed somewhere beyond Cecil, lost again in the labyrinth of his mind.

Cecil had witnessed Spencer's nightmares in the past, but they had never been this violent. Spencer would be out of his head and push or shove Cecil, but he had never gone after him like he did tonight. As usual, the next day Spencer would be apologetic and offer Cecil the money he had panhandled or the lion's share of the food they foraged during the day.

From their first meeting, Cecil felt Spencer needed him and never hesitated to have the older man's back.

Cecil couldn't put his hand on what may have caused the change in Spencer, but it had been over a week since he noticed Spencer's nightmares were more frequent. Spencer had become quieter than usual after he was awake.

Cecil wanted to make sure Spencer was okay. He slowly approached him. Cecil's slight movement caused Spencer to snap out of his trance.

In Spencer's waking dream, Cecil appeared as a man without a face looming above him. Spencer lashed out at his opponent, determined to give as good as he got against the phantom who sought to end his life.

Cecil, caught off guard, did his best to fend off a crazed Spencer who no longer recognized him. In a split second, it dawned on Cecil that Spencer was fighting for his life, and he, in turn, would have to fight for his own. Cecil's survivor mode kicked in, and he no longer tried to avoid Spencer's attack but launched himself into his full-on attack.

CHAPTER 3

The security office was quiet, except for the soft hum of the monitors lining the wall. **Devona Drummond**, 38-year-old African American man magnet, leaned casually against the desk. Her sharp eyes scanned the screens as she spoke. "You know I don't mind holding down the fort while you handle your business," she said, her tone light but reassuring.

The Guard, a burly man with a weary expression, gave her an apologetic smile. "I hate to pull you away from your desk," he replied, his voice tinged with gratitude. "I know if you're here this late, it's important, but George called out, and Phyllis is MIA."

Devona waved a dismissive hand, her lips curving into a small smile. "Take your time. I brought my laptop with me, so I can get some work done."

The guard nodded, clearly relieved, and stepped out the door, leaving Devona alone in the room. The door clicked shut behind him, and the quiet settled in once more.

She turned her attention to the monitors, her gaze flitting across the various feeds. Grainy black-and-white footage displayed different areas of the hospital grounds—the main entrance, the emergency bay, and the parking lot. Her eyes lingered on a particular feed for a moment: a camera capturing the alley adjacent to the hospital's loading dock.

The alley was dimly lit, the harsh glow of a single streetlamp illuminating a narrow stretch of cracked pavement. Something about the scene caught her attention. There were two bums in the alley scuffling.

Not giving the scene a second thought, she placed her laptop on the desk and opened it. The faint glow of the screen adding a soft blue tint to the room. She began typing, the rhythmic clicking of the keyboard blending with the hum of the monitors.

But every so often, her eyes flicked back to the screen showing the alley. The bums scuffling had become more intense.

The fading evening light barely reached the alley beside Mercy Hospital, leaving it cloaked in deep shadows. **Simetra Thomas** stepped into the narrow space, her heels clicking softly against the pavement. She cradled two to-go boxes in her hands, their warmth seeping through the thin Styrofoam.

Simetra, African American, in her early 40's and with a presence that commanded attention, glanced around the alley as she walked. Her sharp eyes immediately caught sight of the commotion ahead. Two men— Spencer and Cecil—were locked in a chaotic struggle, their shoves and wild gestures breaking the usual quiet of the alley.

"Spence, Cecil, what's going on here?" Simetra called out, her voice firm but tinged with concern.

Neither man stopped. Spencer lunged, his scarred face twisted with a mix of desperation and anger, while

Cecil shoved back, his younger frame straining to hold his ground.

Simetra's brow furrowed, and without hesitation, she stepped toward them, determined to break up the fight. She tried to wedge herself between the two men, her free hand outstretched as she said, "Enough, both of you!"

The scuffle didn't stop. In the ensuing chaos, an errant shove sent her off balance. She stumbled, her feet catching on uneven pavement, and fell hard to the ground. The to-go boxes hit first, the contents spilling onto the grimy alley floor, forgotten in the moment.

"Dammit!" Simetra hissed, her hands splaying against the ground to push herself up. But the sight of Spencer's wild expression made her freeze for just a moment.

Her heart thudded in her chest as she reached for her phone, fumbling to unzip her crossbody bag. The strap dug into her shoulder as her fingers searched for the familiar shape of the device. "Stop it!" she shouted, her voice sharp as she tried to command their attention.

The tension in the alley was suffocating; the air was thick with the sounds of shoving, grunting, and ragged breaths. Simetra's fingers finally closed around her phone, but as she pulled it free, her mind raced with what to do next.

The soft glow of the monitors cast shadows across the small guard shack. Devona sat at the desk, her laptop open, but her attention shifted to one of the security feeds on the wall. Her eyes narrowed as she focused on the screen.

The footage showed Simetra Thomas sprawled on the ground, her clothes smeared with food. Above her, two homeless men shoved and grappled with one another, their movements erratic and uncontrolled.

Devona leaned back in her chair, a faint smirk tugging at the corner of her lips. "This witch is finally getting what she deserves," she muttered under her breath.

She reached for the control panel and paused the footage, the image freezing on Simetra's disheveled figure. Devona's fingers moved deftly across the controls as she rewound the video, watching the scuffle play out again from the start. Her eyes gleamed with quiet satisfaction as the chaos unfolded.

Then, with a single decisive click, she deleted the footage. The screen flickered briefly before going blank, and Devona reached for the camera's controls. Her hand hovered for a moment before cutting the feed entirely, ensuring no further recording would take place.

Turning her attention to the guard station's computer, Devona pulled it toward her. She tapped on the keyboard, her movements quick and purposeful, until she found what she was looking for: a video of two maintenance workers carrying boxes away from the hospital's loading dock. The timestamp matched earlier in the evening.

Devona pulled a thumb drive from her pocket, its metallic surface catching the faint light. She inserted it into the computer and dragged the video file onto the drive. The progress bar moved swiftly, and once the transfer was complete, she deleted the file from the system with a few swift keystrokes.

The guard shack fell silent, save for the faint hum of the equipment. Devona removed the thumb drive, turning it over in her hand before slipping it into her pocket. She glanced once more at the blank monitor where Simetra's struggles had played out moments ago.

Satisfied, Devona closed her laptop and leaned back in her chair, her expression calm and composed. Whatever game she was playing, she had just ensured she held the upper hand.

The door to the guard shack creaked open, letting in a faint draft of night air. Devona didn't look up from her laptop until the sound of footsteps stopped just inside. The guard stood there, leaning casually against the doorframe, his broad shoulders filling the space.

Without a word, he crossed the room and pulled Devona into an embrace, his hands settling possessively around her waist. She allowed herself to melt into his hold, tilting her head slightly as his fingers traced lazy patterns up her thigh.

"You weren't too bored while I was gone, were you?" he murmured, his voice low and teasing.

Devona smirked, her lips curving into a playful grin. "I was just a little," she replied, her tone light and suggestive. "But you can make it up to me now that you're back."

Her hand drifted to the light switch, and with a single flick, the room was plunged into shadow.

CHAPTER 4

The hospital parking lot was mostly empty, the stillness broken only by the occasional sound of a car engine in the distance. **Nevell Carter** sat in the back of Simetra's SUV, the tailgate propped open. A first aid kit lay open beside him, its contents neatly arranged.

Simetra perched on the edge of the tailgate, her arm extended toward Nevell. He worked with careful precision, cleaning a scrape on her arm. The sting of antiseptic brought a slight wince to her face, but she didn't complain.

"How many times have I told you not to be so trusting of these street people?" Nevell said, his tone was a mix of exasperation and concern.

Simetra rolled her eyes, her lips curving into a faint smile. "It's just a scratch, Bubba. I'm alright."

Nevell paused, lifting his eyes to meet hers. "Still like when we were kids," he said with a sigh. "Always making light of it when you get hurt."

"You haven't changed either," Simetra shot back, her voice warm but teasing. "Still making too much of other people's pain."

Nevell chuckled softly, shaking his head as he unwrapped a bandage. "Not everybody's pain," he said, his voice softening. "I only make a big deal out of it when you get hurt."

Simetra's smile deepened, a flicker of nostalgia passing between them. "I could always depend on you to rescue me," she said, her voice quieter now, laced with genuine affection.

"That's because I've always been a sucker when you would holler for help," Nevell replied, smoothing the bandage over her arm. He sat back, his gaze lingering on her. "This... whatever you want to call it, is so unnecessary."

Simetra tilted her head, studying him with the same familiar fondness. "Maybe," she said softly. "But I'm glad you're here anyway."

Nevell begins to pack away the first aid supplies, his movements unhurried. "Somebody's gotta watch out for you," he said. "I always have, always will."

Simetra laughed softly, shaking her head. "Still the same Bubba," she said. "And I wouldn't have it any other way." Nevell inspects his handiwork while removing food from Simetra's hair. "I don't want to hear about this happening again," said Nevell, his voice stern. "Especially with those two guys from tonight."

Simetra crossed her arms, leaning slightly against the edge of the tailgate as she fixed Nevell with a firm gaze. "So, I shouldn't try to provide a free meal to someone who might go to sleep hungry? The hospital is throwing the food away, for God's sake."

Nevell sighed. "Sis, even you can't be naive enough to believe that all these people want is a meal and a place to sleep," he said, his tone a mix of caution and frustration.

"Spence and Cecil are harmless," Simetra replied with conviction. "I've been bringing them leftovers for over a month now."

Nevell shook his head, his lips pressing into a thin line. "I know you want to hang on to Mom's tradition of feeding people all over the world," he said, his voice softening, "but I really wish you'd stop doing this, Sis. Why don't you stick to fighting for the rights of your patients when it comes to their bills? That's pretty badass if you ask me."

Simetra arched a brow, a sly smile tugging at her lips. "That's your nice way of saying I can't cook for shit?"

Nevell laughed, a short, warm sound as he closed the first aid kit. "Pretty much about the cooking," he admitted, "but I meant it as a compliment."

Simetra chuckled, shaking her head. "I can't remember the last time you gave me a compliment. Let me not jinx it and have you take it back."

"All jokes aside," Nevell said, his tone turning serious, "take this to heart, Sis. You're good at handing out these leftovers, but what if someone tries to rob you? Or worse?" He met her eyes, his expression earnest. "If you're going to let them get that close, you need to at least be able to defend yourself."

Simetra's smile faded slightly as she absorbed his words. There was truth in his concern, and despite her instincts to brush it off, she couldn't deny the reality he was pointing out.

"I hear you, Bubba," she said finally, her tone soft but resolute. "I can't just stop caring about people. It's not who I am."

Nevell nodded, his face thoughtful as he closed the SUV's tailgate. "I know," he said quietly. "Just promise me you'll be careful, alright?"

"I promise," Simetra said, the hint of a smile returning as she reached out to squeeze his shoulder. "Thanks for patching me up. You're still the best big brother a girl could ask for."

Nevell grinned. "Damn right I am."

CHAPTER 5

The psych ward at Mercy Hospital in Newport News, Virginia, was eerily silent except for the faint hum of machinery. Spencer Walach lay restrained on the table, his eyes darting toward the ceiling, wide with panic. His breathing was frantic, his muffled screams trapped behind the bit strapped tightly in his mouth.

Nurse **Carla Benyon** glanced at her watch, her movements brisk and methodical. At twenty-five, Carla was seasoned enough to handle the ward's grim routines, though she rarely let it show when the strain got to her. She checked the connections to the electroshock machine, ensuring everything was in place.

A noise outside in the hallway drew her attention. She straightened and turned toward the door, her brow furrowed. "Hello?" she called out, her voice steady but curious.

No response. The hallway beyond was empty, its fluorescent lights casting long, sterile shadows. Carla hesitated, her eyes narrowing as she scanned the space. Then, with a small shake of her head, she stepped back into the room and refocused on her task.

Spencer's muffled screams grew louder, more desperate. "Mmmm, Umph!!! Mummm, Umph!!!" he cried, his body trembling against the restraints.

"Justin, where are you?" Carla called over her shoulder, her voice sharp now with annoyance.

Still no answer.

Her finger hovered over the machine's switch, tension building in the room like a static charge. Before she could proceed, the door creaked open behind her. Carla turned quickly, startled by the intrusion.

A man stepped into the room, his tool chest in hand. He wore a worn utility uniform, his name badge identifying him as **Ray Stewart.**

Ray's eyes flicked briefly to Spencer, strapped to the table, before settling on Carla. He offered an apologetic smile. "What are you doing in here?" Carla demanded, her tone laced with irritation.

Ray raised his hands slightly, a gesture of harmlessness. "I'm sorry, ma'am," he said, his voice calm. "Didn't know anyone was in here. I made some repairs in this room earlier and left a few tools behind."

Carla's expression softened slightly, but her posture remained rigid. She gestured toward the table. "This is hardly the time for maintenance to be in here."

"It'll only take a second," Ray said quickly, his gaze darting around the room as though searching for something. He slipped past Carla with a practiced ease. He balanced his tool chest on one hip. "Ma'am, I'll be out of your way in no time."

Carla watched him carefully, suspicion flickering in her eyes. She said nothing as Ray knelt to search the area near the door. Spencer's muffled screams continued in the background, a haunting reminder of the moment's gravity.

Carla knew she was breaking the hospital rules by letting this Stewart guy into the treatment room while the treatment was in progress. She couldn't be blamed, though. He'd barged right into the suite without knocking. She just wanted him to get out.

"Where is Justin when I need him right now?"

Ray grabbed the last of his tools, glancing once more at Spencer as he straightened up. His gaze lingered for a second too long, drawing a wary look from Carla. She crossed her arms, her suspicion evident. Without a word, Ray offered a quick nod and slipped out of the room, the door clicking softly shut behind him.

Carla let out a small huff, turning her attention back to the electroshock machine. Her finger hovered over the switch when the door suddenly burst open.

"Don't do it!"

Carla jumped, her hand flying to her chest. "What's wrong with you, fool?!" she snapped, glaring at **Justin Ambrose** as he stumbled into the room, all dramatic flair and urgency. "You almost made me electrocute this man!"

Justin, a wiry young man with boundless energy, threw up his hands in exasperation. "I should be asking *you* what's wrong with *you!*" he shot back, his tone incredulous. "Why would you administer a shock treatment alone?"

Carla's eyes narrowed, her irritation growing. "I wouldn't *be* alone if you were where you were supposed to be," she retorted. "Where were you, anyway?"

Justin sighed, already pulling on a pair of gloves. "I was in 216 with Bosworth," he said, exhaling sharply. "He pulled a Houdini and got out of his restraints again."

Carla rolled her eyes, muttering under her breath about the ward's endless chaos.

Meanwhile, Justin stepped around her, moving toward Spencer. His demeanor shifted, becoming more focused and professional as he adjusted the electrodes on Spencer's head. "Let me double-check these," he murmured, ensuring everything was in place.

Spencer's muffled whimpers grew louder, his wide eyes flicking between the two nurses. Justin gave him a brief, reassuring look, though it did little to ease the man's evident terror.

"Next time, Carla," Justin said, his voice calmer now, "wait for backup. Even if I'm busy playing escape artist wrangler, don't do this on your own. You know the protocol."

Carla crossed her arms, her expression softening slightly. "Fine," she muttered, her earlier defensiveness giving way to a reluctant acknowledgment. "But next time, don't leave me hanging."

Justin smirked. "Deal. Now, let's finish this up before anything else decides to go sideways today."

Carla nodded, and together, they turned their attention back to Spencer, the room settling into an uneasy stillness once more.

Justin adjusted the electrodes one final time and glanced at Carla. "Just a gentle reminder," he said with a wry smile, "this place might be called Mercy, but if anything goes wrong up here, they ain't gonna have mercy on either one of us."

Carla huffed, though a hint of nervousness flickered across her face. "You know me. I'm not trying to get in trouble," she said defensively. "But if I don't get this treatment done on time, the next shift's charge nurse will be all up my behind. You *know* she doesn't like me."

Justin chuckled softly, shaking his head. "Well, I'm here now. Let's fire this baby up."

Carla exhaled sharply, her nerves still frayed from the earlier commotion. She stepped toward the machine, her fingers brushing the switch. With a determined flick, she threw it.

Nothing happened.

Carla frowned, her brow furrowing. "What the...?" she muttered, throwing the switch again.

She heard Justin scream behind her. Then she felt a surge of electricity engulf her body.

Carla's scream tore through the room, high and piercing. She stumbled backward, her hands flying to her face as the scene unfolded in a horrifying blur.

Before she lost consciousness, she saw sparks fly, illuminating the room in bursts of white light.

A loud crackling sound erupted from the machine, sharp and menacing. Spencer's body spasmed violently on the table, his muffled cries turning into strangled, gut-wrenching sounds. His limbs jerked uncontrollably as the machine sputtered and hissed.

The smell of burning wires filled the air, acrid and suffocating.

Then, as suddenly as it had begun, everything went black.

The hum of the electroshock machine died, and the room plunged into an oppressive silence. Spencer's body lay unmoving.

Carla and Justin both began to stir, confused as to what just happened in the darkened room.

CHAPTER 6

The business office at Mercy Hospital was quiet, save for the soft tapping of keys as Devona Drummund rummaged through the files on the desk. Papers were scattered haphazardly, and the soft glow of the desktop computer illuminated her determined, mocha-colored face.

With a few more keystrokes, she was in. The screen flickered, revealing the information she sought. Devona's focus was razor-sharp—until a sound behind her made her freeze.

"Uh, uh, hmm!"

Devona's head snapped up to see Simetra Thomas standing in the doorway, arms crossed, and eyebrows raised.

Devona plastered on a sheepish grin, her fingers scrambling to shut off the computer. She quickly rebooted it, the screen going dark just as Simetra stepped into the room.

"And why," Simetra began, her tone sharp and cutting, "are you on *my* desk? You know how I feel about people touching my things—*especially* you.”

Devona straightened, smoothing her skirt nervously. “Uh! I was looking for some papers for Mr. Colton,” she said, forcing a note of sincerity into her voice. “I tried to find them myself. I didn’t know how long you would be away. I apologize.”

Simetra’s eyes narrowed. “Apology not accepted,” she said flatly, moving further into the room. “Nothing is ever that simple with you. Now, what did you *really* come in here for?”

Devona’s smile faltered, but she quickly recovered. “I wouldn’t lie!” she said, a hint of indignation creeping into her voice. “Scott asked me to ask you for your file on a patient.”

Simetra’s lips pressed into a thin line. “He’ll be strong,” she muttered, brushing past Devona to walk around her desk.

Devona moved quickly, jumping up and darting out from behind the desk before Simetra could corner her. She hovered near the door, watching as Simetra sat down and took stock of her workspace.

Simetra's eyes landed on her desktop screen, now rebooting. Her expression darkened, suspicion flaring in her gaze as she looked back at Devona.

"What exactly were you doing on my computer?" Simetra asked coldly, her tone leaving no room for evasion.

Devona raised her hands defensively. "Nothing! Like I said, just looking for those papers for Mr. Colton. That's all."

Simetra didn't reply. Instead, she continued to eye Devona with a hard, calculating stare that seemed to strip away any pretense.

The tension hung heavy in the air as the computer finished rebooting. Whatever Devona had been up to, it was clear Simetra wasn't buying her story.

Seeing that Simetra didn't believe a word she said, Devona plastered on a fake pout.

"I didn't mean to, but I accidentally bumped your computer and unplugged it. I was just turning it back on when you came in."

Simetra leaned back in her chair, her eyes never leaving Devona. Her voice was cool and measured as she asked, "Who is the patient?"

Devona hesitated, shifting her weight from one foot to the other. "Spencer Walach," she finally replied, her tone carefully neutral.

Simetra's brow furrowed. "Scott can access this patient's records," she said, her words clipped and matter-of-fact. "Why does he want my hard file?"

Devona tilted her head, a faint glimmer of something unreadable in her expression. "Haven't you heard about what happened to Mr. Walach?"

Simetra's stomach tightened. "No," she said slowly. "What happened to Mr. Walach?"

Devona's voice dropped to a near whisper, her words hanging ominously in the air. "He's dead."

The room fell silent, the revelation settling between them like a dense fog.

Simetra stared at Devona, her mind racing. Whatever game Devona was playing, it was clear the stakes had just been raised.

CHAPTER 7

Detective **Levi Stone**, a man in his mid-forties with a hardened demeanor, sat behind his cluttered desk. He opened a manila envelope, tilting it to spill its contents onto the surface.

A single photograph slid out first, its edges slightly curled. Levi picked it up, his sharp eyes narrowing as he studied the grim image of a man's charred remains. He was barely recognizable. Bold writing scrawled across the top of the photo read: Spencer Walach.

There was a second photo of a machine that was badly burned. Levi had no idea what it could be.

Levi frowned, his jaw tightening. He set the photo aside and reached back into the envelope. His fingers brushed against the rough surface of the paper. He unfolded it carefully, revealing a cryptic note:

TIC TOK. TIME IS RUNNING OUT. YOU'LL FIND THE ANSWERS AT MERCY HOSPITAL.

Levi's eyes scanned the note twice, his expression darkening. He let out a sharp breath, tossing the note onto his desk beside the photo.

Reaching for the phone, he punched in a number from memory. The line buzzed briefly before a male voice answered.

"Yeah, it's Stone," Levi said, his voice low and commanding. "I need the name of whoever's in charge over at Mercy Hospital. Yeah, I'll wait."

He leaned back in his chair, his fingers drumming against the desk. His gaze drifted back to the note, the words "TIME IS RUNNING OUT" glaring back at him like a warning.

Levi snapped pictures of the envelope's contents on his phone, his fingers steady despite the adrenaline coursing through him. He uploaded them to his computer, ensuring a backup was created, and then…

Levi opened the pictures on his computer. The gruesome images jumped off the screen—deep lacerations, dark burn marks, and something worse he couldn't quite put into words. His stomach twisted. What the hell had happened to this poor bastard?

More importantly, who had sent him the envelope with damning evidence, and why?

With a measured breath, he picked up the phone on his desk and dialed a familiar number. The line connected instantly, as if the person on the other end had been expecting his call.

"Get back in here, Shepherd," Levi ordered, his voice firm. "Bring a pair of gloves for me and a pair for yourself. I can't afford any mistakes."

Levi hung up. Within minutes, **Greg Shepherd**, a twenty-three-year-old rookie, appeared hesitantly in the doorway. His sheepish expression and slow approach toward Levi's desk betrayed his apprehension. Levi had called him out earlier, and Shepherd had no desire to land in his bad graces twice in one day.

Shepherd had been relegated to desk duty after prematurely discharging his weapon during a convenience store robbery. The cashier behind the register had been injured as a result. He did his best to keep a low profile, but Stone made sure that staying under the radar wasn't an option.

Levi took the gloves Shepherd offered and snapped them on. "Where did you get this envelope?" he asked.

"I found it near a trash bin in the lobby," Shepherd responded. "It was addressed to you, sir, so I brought it to you right away."

Levi examined the envelope more closely, running a gloved finger over the rough paper. No return address, no identifying marks. There was just his name scrawled across the front in an unsteady hand. Whoever had left it wanted to remain anonymous, but they also wanted him to see what was inside.

He glanced up at Shepherd, who shifted uncomfortably under his scrutiny. "Was anybody around when you found the envelope?" "Not that I remember," said Shepherd. "Did anyone see you pick it up?"

Shepherd hesitated, then shook his head. "Not that I noticed. But the lobby's got cameras. We could check the footage."

"Get me that footage ASAP," Levi instructed, motioning toward Shepherd's gloves. "Put them on." He handed the envelope over. "Take this to forensics. I want the envelope and the contents dusted for prints. Have them check for any trace evidence—fibers, DNA, anything they can find."

Shepherd nodded, carefully handling the envelope as if it might explode. "Understood, sir. I'll get on it right away."

Levi leaned back in his chair, exhaling slowly. His gut told him this was just the beginning of something much bigger. The person who sent that envelope wanted his attention—and they had it.

CHAPTER 8

Levi Stone leaned across the polished surface of **Scott Colton's** desk. He extended his hand toward Colton, a sharp-dressed man in his mid-forties with the air of someone who was always juggling too much.

"Detective Levi Stone, Newport News PD," Levi introduced himself, his voice steady and professional. "I really appreciate you taking the time to talk to me. I know how busy you are, running a hospital and all."

Colton hesitated before taking Levi's hand, his smile practiced. "I always have time for the police department," he replied smoothly, releasing the handshake. "But I'm not sure how I can help."

Levi reached into his leather folder and pulled out the photograph of Spencer Walach's charred remains. He placed it on the desk, sliding it toward Colton.

Colton's expression hardened as he glanced at the photo, his eyes briefly flickering over the grisly image. He sighed heavily, rolling his eyes in a gesture of irritation rather than shock.

"What is this?" Colton asked, his tone bordering on dismissive.

Levi's gaze didn't waver. "This is Spencer Walach," he said, his voice cool. "The note I received suggests I'd find answers to his death here. Care to explain?"

Colton glanced at the clock on his desk, the faintest hint of impatience crossing his face. "Detective, this hospital sees hundreds of patients every day. I don't personally oversee every case, and I have no idea what this has to do with us."

Levi leaned in closer, his tone taking on an edge. "Then I suggest you make some time to figure it out."

Levi Stone's sharp gaze stayed fixed on Scott Colton as he leaned back slightly, his voice taking on a measured tone. "It isn't every day the police receive a tip about a crime committed at this hospital. Do you know anything about this?"

Before Colton could respond, the phone on his desk rang, the shrill sound breaking the tense silence. Both men startled slightly, though Colton recovered quickly. He reached for the phone, putting on a professional demeanor.

"Ms. Drummond," Colton said curtly, "I'm with someone right now. I'll call you right back." Without waiting for a reply, he ended the call and set the receiver down, turning his attention back to Levi.

"Where were we?" Colton asked, feigning composure. "Ah, yes. I don't know where you got this," he gestured toward the photograph Levi had shown him earlier, "but if this did take place at the hospital, our hands are tied because of HIPAA laws. No one from this hospital can discuss a patient without a court order."

Levi's expression darkened, his patience thinning. "That is a bunch of BS," he retorted bluntly.

Before Colton could respond, his phone rang again. With an irritated sigh, he hit a button, silencing the ringer and activating the Do Not Disturb mode.

Colton shifted in his seat, the nervous energy now visible in his fidgeting hands. "You know as well as I do," he said hastily, "that next of kin must file a formal complaint to open a police investigation."

Levi leaned forward, his voice calm but unyielding. "Yes, Mr. Colton, I'm aware of that. That's why I'm curious why no one is asking questions about what happened to this patient."

He reached into his folder, pulling out another document, and slid it across the desk toward Colton. The tension in the room thickened as Colton glanced down at the folder, his face pale.

Scott Colton pulled the photograph of Spencer Walach's charred body from the folder, studying it for a moment, his jaw clenched tight. His eyes flicked over to the clock on his desk, noting the time as if it held some significance. The quiet ringing of his phone seemed louder now, the multiple lines lighting up despite it being silent.

Levi Stone's voice broke through the tension. "This was sent to me anonymously. That person thinks this guy's death is worth investigating."

Scott's face twisted into a grimace, his seething frustration evident as he gritted his teeth. He set the photo down and finally spoke, his voice carefully controlled. "Detective, I assure you the hospital has investigated Mr. Walach's case. All findings point to his death being accidental."

Levi's response was sharp, unyielding. "From speaking with some of your staff, I found out that this patient managed to get himself electrocuted during a procedure."

Scott's temper flared. His hands balled into fists. "Where do you get off speaking to my staff without clearing it with me or my corporate office first?"

Levi didn't flinch. "It wasn't like I formally questioned them. I just showed them the picture. They supplied the rest of the information voluntarily."

Scott's nostrils flared as he stood up abruptly, his body language dismissive. "I think we're done here. Come back when you have a warrant." He waved toward the door. " This conversation is over," his voice final.

Levi stood his ground, meeting Scott's gaze with unwavering resolve. "You can count on it."

The words lingered in the air as Levi turned and walked out, the door closing behind him with a sharp click.

Scott picked up the phone with one hand, his eyes still locked on where Levi had been standing, as he punched a button with the other. "Devona, find out who has talked with the cops about Spencer Walach and fire their ass."

CHAPTER 9

The door to Simetra's office flew open without a knock. Scott Colton strode in, his presence swallowing the room as he loomed over her desk.

Simetra straightened instinctively, locking eyes with him.

"I need everything you have on Mr. Walach," Scott said, skipping pleasantries.

She raised a single, unimpressed eyebrow. "Why my file?"

Scott leaned in, his voice a quiet command. "Because you're thorough. I need everything buttoned up."

Simetra's expression remained unreadable, but a flicker of something crossed her eyes. "I heard his death was accidental. Shouldn't be much to button up."

Scott's jaw tightened. "Seriously, Ms. Thomas," he said, his tone edged with ice. "Do your job. And mind your business."

Simetra didn't flinch. Instead, she held his gaze, her silence a quiet rebellion.

Simetra's gaze remained steady, her voice cool but firm. "Is that a threat? I know you're used to intimidating everyone around here, but I don't take kindly to being strong-armed."

Scott's lips curled into a slow, predatory smile. "That's what I like about you, Ms. Thomas. You never miss an opportunity to remind me of my boundaries."

He lowered himself into the chair across from her, his posture still imposing. Simetra didn't so much as blink. Instead, she reached for a file on her desk, sliding it toward him with deliberate calm.

Her expression gave nothing away, but the slight pause before she let go spoke volumes.

"Mr. Colton, I don't care if you like me or not," Simetra said, her voice steady. "Either way, I'm not intimidated by you."

Scott's grin widened, devoid of warmth. "I would never try to intimidate you, Ms. Thomas," he said smoothly, his tone dipping into something colder, more calculating. "But let's not forget—I'm your boss. Not the other way around."

He reached for the file, flipping through the pages with a lazy flick of his wrist, as if whatever was inside barely warranted his attention.

Simetra didn't look away, her gaze steady, unyielding.

Scott skimmed the file, then leveled a sharp gaze at Simetra. "Is this everything?"

She gave a measured nod. "That's all I have. His file says he was indigent. No next of kin, no guarantor. What should I do about his bill?"

Scott's expression hardened, impatience flickering beneath the surface. "The hospital's going to have to eat the fees. You have my authorization to waive the costs. The sooner we close the book on this case, the better."

Simetra's eyes narrowed. "Why the rush? What happened?"

Scott hesitated, just for a second, his jaw tightening before he spoke. "I don't know the details, but the staff wasn't at fault."

Simetra leaned back, arms crossing, skepticism written in every line of her posture. "And you're not going to look into it? Because he was poor? Because he was homeless?"

Scott's voice sharpened, his response immediate. "Before you climb up on your soapbox, let's be real—he couldn't afford the treatment anyway."

Simetra's eyes flashed, her disbelief turning to something closer to anger. "You can't be serious."

Scott held her gaze, his tone flat, unwavering. "Dead serious. What happened to Walach was unfortunate, but it can't be undone. We'll be lucky if our in-house investigation is enough to prove that, tragic or not, this was an accident."

Simetra sat stiffly, her fingers curling around the edge of her desk. The air between them grew thick, charged with something unspoken.

Scott snatched up the files from Simetra's desk before she could reach them.

"Wait a minute! Those are my files!" Simetra yelled.

Scott didn't stop. He strode toward the door, files in hand. *"I'll give them back when I'm done."*

Scott Colton prided himself on being in control.

Back in his office, Scott Colton stared at the file on his desk, his pulse pounding in his ears. Simetra had been too thorough—too damn good at her job. The neatly compiled pages in front of him weren't just records. They were a noose tightening around his neck.

Buried in medical reports, timestamps, and security logs was a clear pattern. One that led straight to him.

His fingers clenched around the file. This wasn't just suspicion. It was evidence.

A slow exhale left his lips as he leaned back in his chair, jaw tightening. The file had to disappear. And so did Simetra Thomas.

The office was dim, shadows stretching long across the walls as the steady hum of a paper shredder filled the silence.

Scott Colton sat behind his desk, methodically feeding page after page into the machine. The shredder whirred, its rhythm cold and mechanical, chewing through the damning evidence in his hands.

His face remained unreadable, but his fingers twitched—just once—as another sheet disappeared between the blades. A sharp *click* echoed as the mechanism reset, followed by the soft rustle of shredded remains falling into the bin below.

Scott exhaled slowly, eyes locked on the pile of paper strips. Pieces of a case that could ruin him. Fragments of a person's truth— now nothing more than waste.

The glow of his desk lamp cast an eerie light across his face, sharpening the hard set of his jaw.

This was necessary. He hated loose ends. Simetra Thomas was now a loose end he had to eliminate.

Scott Colton pulled up a screen on his desktop computer and selected a video file. The footage flickered to life, revealing a live feed from Simetra's office. In silence, Simetra inserted a jump drive and began transferring a file.

Scott leaned back in his chair, resting his feet on the desk. He folded his arms behind his head.

"Ah, Simetra, what are you up to now?" he mused aloud.

On the screen, Simetra glanced around, her movements wary, as if she sensed unseen eyes on her. The files continued to upload.

She spoke into the empty office. *"I don't know why Scott wants my hard data. Something feels off. I don't trust that guy for a second."*

The file finally finished uploading. Simetra grabbed her purse, slipped the jump drive inside, and shut down the computer. She walked to the office door, paused for a final glance at her desk, then switched off the light.

Scott bolted upright from his relaxed

position, slamming his fist onto the desk.

CHAPTER 10

Early morning in Nevell's home gym, Simetra's fists struck the heavy bag with dull, unfocused thuds. Her punches were weak, lacking precision. Sweat trickled down her forehead, her breath coming in shallow bursts.

Nevell stood off to the side, arms crossed, watching her with a mix of concern and determination.

"You've got to hit harder than that," taunted Nevell. "Those punches aren't going to get anybody off you." Simetra scoffed, exasperated, pausing to wipe sweat from her brow.

"Do you even know what you're doing?" asked Simetra. For the last half hour, you've done nothing but torture me." Nevell stepped closer, his voice calm but firm, closing the distance between them.

Nevell sports a wide grin as he challenges Simetra. "This is based purely on what I learned from YouTube, but looking at you, your punches need to be tighter to be effective."

"Okay, smarty pants," challenged Simetra.

"You can't just go through the motions. You've got to put everything into it, or else it's all for nothing." He raised his hands, the pads now ready. "Come on, let's see what you've got."

Simetra huffed, frustration creeping into her voice. Nevell raised his hands. "Come on, hit the pads." Simetra adjusted her stance and began alternating jabs and punches against his gloves.

Simetra hisses through clenched teeth, "This better be worth it, Bubba." Nevell watches her carefully, nodding in approval with each punch. "That's more like it. Keep going."

Simetra's breathing steadies as she continues, each punch now packed with more focus, each strike echoing through the gym.

"Hold up, hold up," Nevell yelled. Simetra stopped mid-swing, brow furrowed.

Simetra pulled her arms closer to her body, adjusting her form. As she leaned forward to throw a punch, Nevell suddenly tapped her head, a little too hard, with one of the pads.

"Ow!", cried Simetra. Nevell smirked. "Always protect your head."

Simetra shot him a determined scowl. "Watch out who you smack in the head," Simetra warned. "Payback is a mutha—"

Nevell laughs, "Language, Sis! Language! But your energy is better. That's the kind of punch you'll need if you ever run into the guy who dragged you to the ground in that alley."

Simetra's expression darkened. "We'll never meet under those circumstances again." Nevell clenched his jaw, barely containing his anger. "I better never run across him, period," said Nevell, trying to hold back his anger.

The sound of her gloves connecting with the pads fills the room. With each punch, the intensity builds, the rhythm becoming sharper.

Without warning, Simetra swung and landed a solid punch to Nevell's chin. He shook his head before stumbling to his knees.

Nevell blinks in surprise. "What was that—payback?" Simetra grinned, her satisfaction undeniable. "That's part of it. Trust me, there's more to come."

CHAPTER 11

Devona walked down the hallway of Mercy Hospital, an armload of files stacked precariously in her arms. She rounded a corner and collided head-on with a well-dressed, mixed-race man.

File folders flew everywhere. Nevell bent down, gathering several of them. As he looked up, his gaze landed on Devona just as she made a dramatic show of tugging her too-short skirt back down. She faked embarrassment, but the playful glint in her eyes didn't go unnoticed. They exchanged smiles.

Devona purposely softened her voice, "I'm sorry. I didn't see you. But how could I have missed a tall drink of water like you? You stand out in this place." Her eyes lingered on Nevell's face a beat too long. Nevell grins, "No harm done."

"Are you always this forward?" Nevell asked, glancing at Devona's left hand.

"I don't believe in holding back when I see what I want," Devona replied smoothly. "I don't see a ring. Are you in a relationship?"

"That's supposed to be my line."

"You were taking too long to ask."

Nevell sighed. "I'm single. Are you?"

"Unfortunately, yes. But I'm staying single by choice—I've had a lousy track record when it comes to men."

"You just haven't met the right man."

Nevell gathered the rest of the files from the floor and handed them to Devona. She extended her hand toward him.

"It looks like I'm still waiting to meet him. And you are…?"

He shook her hand. "Nevell Carter."

"Nice to meet you, Nevell Carter. I'm Devona. I'm the Administrator's personal assistant, but I'm also the patient advocate and hospital liaison."

"Nice to meet you, Devona. Got a last name?"

"It's Drummond, but nobody calls me by it."

"Are you visiting a patient?"

"Actually, I'm here to see my sister."

Nevell glanced past Devona just as Simetra stepped out of her office. Without hesitation, she walked straight toward him.

"It's about time you got here," Simetra said as they embraced in a loose hug.

Behind them, Devona stood frozen in the hallway, her expression shifting from surprise to disbelief.

"Well, damn," she muttered.

Devona had felt an undeniable vibe from Nevell Carter. He was handsome, and his watch and tie clip screamed money. His warm smile had disarmed her, pulling her out of her usual comfort zone. She would *never* have admitted to a man she'd just met that she was purposely staying single. But with him, the words had just slipped out.

She smirked, recalling the hunger in his eyes when he'd checked her out. The way his gaze lingered on her ass had sent a flutter through her stomach.

And yet—*how dare* he be related to that goody two-shoes bitch, Simetra?

They didn't even look alike. In fact, they couldn't have been more different–night and day. Simetra was dark-skinned, and Nevell was light-skinned. But there they were, hugging like family.

The way Simetra clung to her brother, Devona knew instantly: any chance of something between her and Nevell was *doomed*. Simetra would be *all up in their business*, and there was no way in hell Devona was dealing with that.

Just like that, she dismissed Nevell.

As he followed Simetra into her office, Devona erased him from her mind completely.

CHAPTER 12

Several days passed. Simetra and Nevell were back in Nevell's home gym. Simetra struck his hands in rapid-fire succession, each punch carrying her full strength. She had him backing up.

"Now that's what I'm talking about," Nevell said, grinning. "It's pretty damn cool that you're ambidextrous. Now that you've been working on controlling your punches, I don't think you have to worry about that guy knocking you down anymore."

Simetra exhaled sharply. "I don't have to worry about him knocking me down—or sleeping in an alley—anymore."

Nevell lowered his hands. "Why's that?"

"He was taken to the psych ward for a 72-hour observation," she said, her voice steady but distant. "Two of the doctors recommended electroshock therapy." She hesitated. "He's dead now."

Nevell studied her. "And you've convinced yourself it's your fault."

She swallowed hard. "I *am* the reason he was sent to the psych ward."

Simetra vividly remembered the cop with his knee on Spencer's neck. Spencer struggled to breathe, his gasps sharp and desperate.

She and Cecil stood frozen in the alley, watching in horror.

Simetra stepped forward, her voice tight. "Do you have to be so rough with him?"

"Step back, ma'am!" the cop barked. "What's this got to do with you anyway?"

"I'm the one who called you."

The officer's hand moved to his belt, unbuckling his taser.

"Is that really necessary?" she asked, her heart pounding.

The cop wrestled with Spencer, his breath ragged from exertion. "Ma'am, if you don't step back, I'm going to use this on you."

Simetra hesitated, then took a step back.

The officer let out a breath, dropping the taser. He eased some of the pressure off Spencer's neck, then grabbed his cuffs.

Within moments, Spencer—barely conscious—was restrained.

"He needs to go to Mercy for a psych evaluation," Simetra said.

"Don't worry, ma'am, that's where he's going," the cop replied. "Feel free to meet him over there."

Just like that, the memory dissolved.

Simetra blinked, realizing she was no longer in the alley but back in Nevell's gym.

Nevell placed a reassuring arm around her. "Don't you dare beat yourself up. The guy was violent. It was just a matter of time before he killed someone."

She exhaled, shaking her head. "I still feel responsible. He already had a shitty life. He must have some family out there looking for him. The least I can do is try to find them."

CHAPTER 13

The club was upscale, exuding luxury and exclusivity. Nevell sat at the bar, nursing his drink, his gaze drifting toward the other patrons—until it settled on *her*.

Across the room, Devona Drummond sat at a table, phone in hand. She looked up, catching his stare. Nevell smirked and raised his glass to her.

Devona tilted her head in acknowledgment.

Taking that as an invitation, Nevell made his way over to her table.

"Devona, right?"

She looked up, brow slightly furrowed. "Have we met?"

"Yeah. Outside my sister's office at Mercy Hospital."

Recognition flickered across Devona's face. "Oh, right, your sister is Simetra, the Business Office Manager. I remember now." She flashed a smile. "Nice seeing you again." She gestured toward the seat across from her. "Why don't you join me?"

Nevell sat but quickly noticed Devona's attention shift toward the bar. A **man** sitting there locked eyes with her. Devona winked. The guy broke into a grin.

Nevell scowled, his jaw tightening. His mood darkened as Devona kept smiling at the guy. Irritated, he waved a hand in front of her face.

"Hel-looo?"

Devona blinked and refocused on Nevell. "Is everything alright?"

"Thanks for inviting me to sit down. It's nice to have you join me again." His voice was edged with sarcasm. "I was going to say, after meeting you the other day, I hoped I'd run into you again. But you seemed… distracted."

Devona gave an apologetic smile. "I'm sorry about that. You have my undivided attention."

"Great. Now that I have it, I'd like to get to know you better. Tell me about yourself."

She shrugged. "Not much to tell. As you can see, I'm so single I have to take myself out for a drink."

"I could cure your loneliness."

Devona raised an eyebrow. "What do you have in mind?"

"I can be pretty romantic if you give me a chance."

"Don't tell me you're the type to order champagne and buy me roses."

Nevell smirked. "Wouldn't be a problem if that's what you're into."

"Nice, but a bit boring." Devona snapped her fingers. "I'm looking for a man who can take me from zero to a hundred—*just like that*."

As if on cue, her eyes roamed the club and landed on the guy at the bar again. The man returned her stare, bolder this time.

Nevell clenched his jaw. "I like you, Devona. From the moment I saw you at Mercy, I thought you were just what the doctor ordered—but you're making it real hard for me to look past the fact that you're disrespecting me with this fuck nut at the bar."

The guy overheard.

He stood up and swaggered toward them, oozing cockiness. "What's up, man? Jealous 'cause your woman likes what she sees?"

Nevell scoffed. "*Jealous?* Never."

The guy smirked at Devona. "Baby, lose this wannabe and come hang out with a real man."

He reached for her, but before he could get too close, Nevell was already on his feet.

The guy shoved him.

Big mistake.

Nevell shoved him back—hard—sending him stumbling. The man steadied himself, then swung.

Nevell dodged easily and countered with a swift punch to his nose. The crack was audible. The man hit the floor, out cold.

Without missing a beat, Nevell tossed some bills onto the table and turned toward the door, his patience long gone.

Behind him, Devona snatched up her purse and hurried after him.

"Wait for me!"

The car sat in a shadowed corner of the parking lot, tucked away from prying eyes. The dim glow of a distant streetlamp barely illuminated the fogged-up windows.

Devona moans loudly as she rides Nevell to orgasm. Nevell let his head fall back against the passenger seat, his breath ragged as Devona moved against him.

His hands gripped her hips, holding her close as he shuddered beneath her.

A slow, satisfied smirk spread across his lips. "So… have I redeemed myself from being a bore?"

Devona leaned in, trailing a teasing finger down his chest. "You've made a good start."

CHAPTER 14

Early morning light filtered through the bedroom window, casting a soft glow over the sprawling space. Nevell and Devona lay tangled in the sheets, his arms wrapped around her as they gazed out at the serene view of the Chesapeake Bay.

"Mmm," Devona murmured, nestling closer. "I could get used to this."

Nevell chuckled. "I was thinking the same thing."

Her eyes drifted around the spacious bedroom, the high ceilings, and the breathtaking waterfront view. "I had no idea you had it *like this*."

"I'm not one to brag," Nevell said with a smirk, "but you're not dealing with a slouch."

She propped herself up on one elbow, curiosity flickering in her eyes. "Tell me to mind my business if this is too personal, but… how did you get all this?"

Nevell exhaled, stretching an arm behind his head. "My bio dad left me an inheritance, and I made smart investments."

"*Bio* dad?" Devona raised an eyebrow. "I was wondering why you and your sister had different last names."

"I kept my mother's maiden name, even though my bio dad claimed me."

He rolled to the edge of the king-size bed, swinging his legs over the side. "Enough about my past. I usually start my day with a few laps in the pool. You're welcome to join me."

Devona smirked. "Not this time. I didn't bring a bikini."

Nevell glanced over his shoulder, his eyes glinting with mischief. "No worries. I won't be wearing trunks."

She laughed, shaking her head. "You go ahead and get your swim on. *I* can't wait to get lost in that kitchen of yours. You'll be amazed at my skills."

As soon as Nevell left the room, Devona remained still, listening to his footsteps fade down the hall. She counted the seconds, waiting until she was sure he had reached the indoor pool.

Then she sprang into action.

Slipping out of bed, she wrapped the sheet around her like a robe and padded silently into the hallway. One by one, she peeked into the rooms, curiosity guiding her until she found what she was looking for—a study, complete with a sleek computer setup.

A sly smile crossed her lips.

She slid into the chair, powered up the computer, and let her fingers fly over the keyboard. Her hacking skills were second nature by now, and within moments, she was deep in Nevell's files.

"My... my... my." Her eyes flickered across the screen, taking in the information before her.

Then—footsteps.

Her heart lurched.

She barely had time to shut down the computer before she dove beneath the desk, pressing herself into the shadows.

The door swung open.

Nevell stepped inside, a towel slung low around his waist, water glistening on his skin. He scanned the room, his brow furrowing slightly. But after a moment, he turned and left, closing the door behind him.

Devona exhaled slowly, waiting a beat before slipping out from under the desk. She moved quickly, making her way back into the hall, careful not to run into Nevell.

What she had just found was a game changer. She was amazed at the secrets Nevell was keeping. She knew one thing for sure. Before it was said and done, she was going to find out *more*.

Devona was usually a wiz at cracking tough files, but maneuvering through Nevell's encrypted data felt like navigating a minefield. Every layer she peeled back threatened to set off an unseen trap. She knew she didn't have much time before Nevell noticed she wasn't in the kitchen.

One file in particular caught her eye. She clicked on it—only to trigger an immediate chain reaction. Before she could react, the file erased itself.

"Shit," she muttered.

Nevell would immediately know that someone had been snooping. There was no covering this up.

With a resigned breath, Devona made a decision. She would tell him the truth. She was a hacker, drawn to his cyber toys like a moth to a flame. The challenge had been too tempting to resist.

Suddenly, Nevell appeared in the doorway of his study. His gaze swept over Devona, slow and deliberate, devoid of emotion.

Her pulse quickened. She wasn't sure where she stood with him, and she wasn't sure if he would believe her story. But if he did, it would mean he trusted her. It would mean he wanted her, too.

She took a steadying breath.

Out loud, she echoed the thought. "Here goes nothing," she murmured, stepping toward him.

CHAPTER 15

Simetra sat at her desk, staring at Spencer Walach's file on her desktop screen. "What is it about you that has Scott in such a hurry to close your case?"

A knock at the door was quickly followed by Nevell stepping inside. "Knock, knock. You know what they say about talking to yourself."

Simetra closed the file. "It's fine as long as you don't answer yourself." She leaned back in her chair. "What are you doing here?"

"I came to take you out to lunch."

"That would be nice. Give me a second to send an email to my boss."

Nevell took a seat opposite her as she typed. "I'll shut down my computer and give myself the rest of the day off," he said with a smirk.

Before Simetra could respond, Devona barreled through the office door. "Scott sent me to find out what's holding you up from sending the revised P&Ls for his meeting this afternoon."

"He'll get them when they're done," Simetra said coolly, not looking up from her screen. "Have some respect for yourself and stop acting like Scott's lapdog."

Devona's mouth tightened. "I beg your pardon?"

"You heard me."

"Sis, don't you think that's kind of harsh?" Nevell interjected.

Devona turned toward him, clearly surprised. Her eyes darted between them before settling on Nevell. "I didn't know you had company." She shot him a warning glance, silently urging him to follow her lead.

Nevell picked up on the cue and played along. "Aren't you going to introduce me to your visitor?"

Simetra sighed but relented. "This is my brother, Nevell."

Nevell stood and extended a hand. "Nice to meet you."

Devona hesitated for only a moment before shaking it. "Nice to meet you, too, Nevell. I'm Devona."

Chapter 16

It's late night and inside Chihuaha's Restaurant, the low hum of conversation fills the air, broken by the occasional clatter of dishes and bursts of laughter from the bar. Neon margarita signs cast soft glows of green and pink across the worn wooden booths. A mariachi cover of a pop song plays faintly from overhead speakers.

Nevell sits rigid in his seat, swirling a half-melted gin and tonic, his eyes fixed on the ice in his glass. Across from him, Devona leans back with the relaxed grace of someone completely unaffected, crunching on a chip and dipping it lazily into salsa.

Nevell's voice is quiet, but tense, "What you did in front of my sister today...That was *so* not cool. Devona raises an eyebrow, unfazed, as she licks a smudge of salsa from her thumb. "Introduce me to your visitor?" Nevell asked. "What was that even about?

Devona continues to dip her chips as if Nevell should get over himself. "I've already been introduced to several of your intimate parts. Devona breathes deeply before coming to life with an attitude of her own. "Your sister called me a dog for God's sake," Devona snapped. "What do you think she would call me if she knew we were dating?" Nevell almost chokes in disbelief. "If my sister can't know about us, where do you see us going as a couple?"

Devona takes a quick glance around the room and notices that the atmosphere has become quiet. Devona leans in close to Nevell and drops her voice an octave, "I admit I'm a bit freaked out because I like you so much." Nevell turns his head slightly. The bartender catches his eye. "Yeah…yeah, I know you're not used to being treated well by the men you date."

Devona's phone buzzes. She looks at the screen, then disconnects the call. "If we're going to see where this relationship can go, you need to understand that I run when I'm chased." Nevell sips his drink. "How do you feel about me catching you?" Devona munches a chip, then takes a sip from her glass of water. "For you, I'm willing to slow down. You've turned my head, Nevell Carter. You make me want to belong to someone."

Nevell memorizes Devona's pouty lower lip as he searches her face for sincerity. "I wish I could believe you." "You can," Devona whispered. She immediately takes the defensive. "I don't need to lie." Nevell reaches across the table and strokes her hand. "I'm just messing with you, woman. You need to lighten up. You're too serious." Devona flips her hand from beneath Nevell's, topping his with her blinged-out nails. She gives Nevell's hand a squeeze. "You bring out the best in me, Nevell." Nevell gives her his first genuine smile of the night. "I must admit I haven't had feelings this strong for a woman so quickly before in my life."

Devona reaches for Nevell's drink and finishes it. "Before we get too sappy here, how about I meet you at your place in an hour? I'd really like to see the sun rise over the Chesapeake in the morning." Nevell gives her a wink, "Bet."

Chapter 17

The night was shrouded in darkness, punctuated only by the occasional flicker of streetlights and the distant hum of the city. Traffic was light but fast-paced, a blur of motion and sound that seemed to pulse with the rhythm of the night.

Nevell gripped the steering wheel tightly; his knuckles throbbed with tension. His eyes darted to the rearview mirror, where the ominous silhouette of a dark sedan loomed closer with every passing second.

The sedan's headlights cut through the darkness like twin daggers, bearing down on Nevell with relentless determination. He could feel the adrenaline surging through his veins, a primal instinct to survive kicking in. With a swift maneuver, Nevell's car dodged in and out of traffic, weaving through the lanes with the precision of a seasoned driver.

The sedan followed suit, matching his every move with unnerving accuracy.

Nevell's heart pounded in his chest as he pressed down on the accelerator, the engine roaring in response. He had to outdistance the sedan, and find a way to escape its relentless pursuit.

The speedometer climbed steadily, the needle edging closer to the red zone. He passed other cars in a blur, their drivers honking in protest as he narrowly avoided collision after collision.

Car horns blared, a cacophony of sound that echoed through the night. Nevell's focus was razor-sharp, his mind calculating every move, every turn. He knew he couldn't keep this up forever; the sedan was too close, too determined.

He needed a plan, a way to shake off his pursuer and find safety.

Nevell's thoughts raced as he reached for the car's Bluetooth, dialing Simetra's number. The phone ran, but went straight to voicemail. His breath hitched with emotion as he left a message. "Sis, I know you think I'm a bit of a hard ass and that I don't value what you do. You couldn't be further from the truth."

He never finishes his next sentence. His eyes caught the sedan in the rearview mirror again. The guy from the bar wore an angry snarl, his hands gripping the steering wheel with a ferocity that sent chills down Nevell's spine.

As he approached a sharp bend in the road, Nevell slowed just enough to keep from running off the road, then accelerated again. The sedan closed in on him, smashing into the rear of his car.

Both vehicles barreled through an intersection, the impact jarring Nevell's senses. He sped up, desperate to escape, but out of the darkness, a delivery truck appeared, blindsiding him.

Nevell's car rolled several times before landing upside down. The world spun around him, a chaotic blur of metal and glass. Pain shot through his body, but he forced himself to stay conscious.

He had to survive; had to find a way out of this nightmare.

A **tall man** wearing a mask and a ball cap approached Nevell's overturned car. Nevell is face down on the roof of the vehicle. The driver's side window is shattered where his head hit the glass.

The tall man reaches into the car window, placing a gloved hand over Nevell's nose and mouth, suffocating him.

Panic surged through Nevell as he struggled to breathe, his vision starting to blur. Suddenly, the man from the bar ran toward the scene, yelling, "Hey, what are you doing?"

The man in the ball cap let go of Nevell and jumped back into the delivery truck.

He sped away, leaving Nevell unconscious. The man from the bar stands beside him, his mind racing with confusion and fear.

Chapter 18

The sterile scent of antiseptic filled the air as Simetra entered the ICU at Mercy Hospital. Her heart ached at the sight of her brother, Nevell, lying in a coma, hooked up to a ventilator and several monitors. The faint hum of medical equipment fills the air, a constant reminder of life's fragility.

Simetra's eyes welled with tears as she approached Nevell's bedside. She had always seen him as strong, invincible, but now he looked fragile, vulnerable. A doctor with his back to Simetra stood nearby, reading over Nevell's chart on the bedside computer. His expression was serious, focused.

"How is he?" Simetra asked, her voice trembling.

The doctor turns to face Simetra, his eyes filled with a mixture of sympathy and professionalism. "He's stable for now, but it's too early to tell. We're monitoring him closely."

Simetra nodded, her gaze never leaving Nevell's face.

"I'm Simetra Thomas, Mr. Carter's sister," she said, her voice trembling.

"**David Rossmore**, Mr. Carter's attending physician," the doctor replied, extending his hand.

"Is my brother going to be alright?" Simetra asked, her heart pounding with fear.

Dr. Rossmore sighed, his face etched with concern. "To be honest with you, I wish I could be more optimistic."

Simetra approached Nevell's bed and stood beside Dr. Rossmore. Nevell lay in bed with his left wrist in a cast. Simetra gently touched his fingers, her eyes searching for any sign of response.

"I looked over Mr. Carter's brain scan," Dr. Rossmore continued, his tone somber. "And I'm not going to lie to you. It doesn't look good."

Simetra's breath caught in her throat. She felt a wave of helplessness wash over her. "What can we do?" she whispered, her voice barely audible.

"We're doing everything we can," Dr. Rossmore assured her. "But right now, it's a waiting game. We need to see how he responds to treatment."

"When you say his brain scan doesn't look good, what does that mean?" she asked, her voice barely above a whisper.

"It means that with your brother's type of injury, we can't guarantee if he will ever come out of the coma," Dr. Rossmore explained.

"Pardon me for being in denial, but I believe God," Simetra said, her voice firm with conviction.

"I appreciate your faith, Ms. Thomas, but from my experience with patients like your brother, there is no clear-cut prediction about his recovery," Dr. Rossmore replied gently.

"I'm not going to give up on him. If I need to, I will be here for him every day until he wakes up," Simetra declared, her determination unwavering.

"That's your option. It's all up to how much you value your time," Dr. Rossmore said, his tone neutral.

"No, it's all up to how much I value my blood. For my blood, there is no price I won't pay," Simetra responded, her voice filled with resolve.

Dr. Rossmore nodded, respecting her determination. "We'll continue to do everything we can for him."

Simetra squeezed Nevell's hand gently, her heart filled with hope and determination. "Hang in there, Nevell. We're all waiting for you."

Chapter 19

Levi Stone sat behind his desk, the weight of his responsibilities evident in his furrowed brow. A knock at the door interrupted his thoughts. He looked up to see an officer leading Simetra and another woman into his office.

"This is Miss Thomas. She's here about Mr. Carter," the officer said before turning to leave.

Levi stood up from his desk, extending his hand. "Have a seat, Ms. Thomas. I'm Detective Stone, but I'm comfortable with you calling me Levi."

Simetra found a chair across from Levi's desk and indicated to the woman beside her to take a seat. "Nice to meet you, Detective Stone. This is my best friend, Phyllis Barlow."

Levi walked over to Phyllis and extended his hands to both women. "I wish we were meeting under different circumstances."

He loaded the video of Nevell's car crash on his computer and turned the screen so Simetra could see the footage. Simetra gasped as she watched Nevell's car roll over and over on the screen.

"Your brother was being chased when he entered the intersection. He was hit from the side by a truck he never saw coming," Levi explained.

Simetra's voice trembled as she asked, "What about the person who hit him?"

"The truck was found abandoned. So far, we're investigating who might have been the driver," Levi replied.

Phyllis interjected, her voice filled with concern, "What about the person chasing Nevell?"

Levi sighed, his expression serious. "We're looking into that as well. "We gathered footage from a few nights ago of your brother at a bar where he got into an altercation with a guy. Simetra feels her anger rising. "Where is this guy?" Levi does his best to keep his voice calm. "I can't really discuss the case while the investigation is ongoing, but we have the man in custody. He's facing charges that could include homicide if your brother were to die, heaven forbid."

Simetra jumps up from her seat and gets in Levi's face. "I hope you know that what you just said doesn't make me feel any better."

Levi motions for Simetra to look at the computer screen. "This may make you feel worse. On the screen are Nevell and Devona at a booth in Chihuahua's. "Your brother was drinking, and he wasn't wearing a seat belt."

Simetra glares at Nevell and Devona. "So he had a few drinks, that's not a crime." "We need to get the statement from the woman he was with. We are having a hard time finding her." Phyllis offers to clear things up for Levi. "She's a glorified clerk at Mercy Hospital," said Phyllis. "Her name is Devona Drummond."

Simetra continues to stare at the screen with distaste. "I take it from your reaction, she's not a favorite. "Not even close," said Simetra. Her voice was cold and calculated. "What I can't figure out is how the hell she ended up on a date with my brother?"

Levi swiveled his computer screen back around on the desk, trying to keep a straight face. "A question you might ask him when he wakes up."

Simetra fixed Levi with the coldest stare ever. "I'll add it to the stack. In the meantime, we need to find out who did this."

Simetra's eyes filled with determination. "Nevell deserves justice."

Levi nodded, his resolve matching hers. "We'll do everything we can to get to the bottom of this. I promise you that."

Phyllis hooks her arm in Simetra's and leads her toward the door. "Come on, Meme, let's get out of here. We should really get to the hospital." Levi pulls out one of his cards and gives it to Simetra as he walks them to the door. "I'd appreciate a call when your brother regains consciousness."

Chapter 20

Nevell's hospital room is dimly lit, the soft glow of the bedside lamp casting long shadows across the sterile white walls. The faint hum of medical equipment fills the air, a constant reminder of the fragility of life.

Nevell lies motionless in the bed, his face gaunt, a stark contrast to the vibrant man he was only days ago.

Devona enters the room, her heart pounding with a mix of fear and determination. She looks around to make sure no one is in the room. She approaches Nevell's bedside, her steps hesitant but purposeful.

Leaning over him, she whispers softly, her voice trembling with emotion. "Nevell, baby, can you hear me? She pauses, her eyes scan Nevell's face, which remains deathly still. "I got access to your chart. You're pretty messed up." Her voice breaks slightly, a hint of guilt creeping in.

Devona sits beside Nevell and leans in close. "It's my bad luck you became a vegetable before I could get that ring. For a minute, I could see myself as Mrs. Nevell Carter. But oh well. Those are the breaks."

Suddenly, the door opens and Simetra enters the room. Her eyes narrow as she takes in the scene before her. "What are you doing here?"

Devona stammers, caught off guard. "I was checking on Mr. Carter." Simetra's gaze sharpens, suspicion evident in her eyes. "You look like you were doing more than checking on him. You're all in the bed with him."

Devona is taken aback but quickly recovers, her mind racing to find an explanation. I know how this must look, but I was trying to see if I could get him to respond. I assure you, I meant no harm."

Simetra steps closer, her expression hardening. Simetra remembers the scene of Nevell and Devona in Chihuahua's, how chummy they were. Simetra could feel her fingers tugging on Devona's weaved extensions. It was all she could do not to act on her impulse. "What's going on between you and my brother?"

Devona's heart races, panic rising within her. She's never been a fighter and she can see that Simetra is beyond pissed because her brother is hurt.

Devona forces herself to remain calm, her voice steady but defensive. "I don't know what you mean. I don't really know Mr. Carter."

Simetra folded her arms and fixed Devona with a hard stare. "You were with him the night of the bar fight and the night of the accident. Cut the crap. You know something about him."

Devona's throat tightened. She could feel the weight of Simetra's suspicion pressing down on her, demanding answers. "Before I met Nevell, I never knew a man could like me for me—not just my body," she said, forcing a steadiness into her voice. "He made me feel like he wanted to take care of me."

Simetra's gaze narrowed. "That's not what I asked. You're dodging."

"I'm not." Devona's pulse was hammering now. She had to hold her ground. "Nevell was different."

Simetra stepped closer, her voice low and sharp. "No. You're twisting this. First, you say you barely knew him. Now, you talk like he was your savior. What aren't you telling me?"

Devona faltered, searching for an escape, but Simetra wasn't letting up. "I… I think if we had more time, I could have fallen for him."

Simetra let out a sharp, mocking laugh. "Unbelievable. That's what you're going with?"

Devona straightened, trying to keep the tremor out of her voice. "Why does it matter?"

"Because you're lying," Simetra said, her voice cold and final. "And that means you're hiding something. Get the hell out."

Devona opened her mouth to protest, but Simetra's expression had hardened into something immovable.

"Now," Simetra said, voice like steel.

CHAPTER 21

Inside Nevell's hospital room, Simetra slumped over his bed, her fingers curled around his limp hand. The rhythmic hum of machines filled the air, a hollow comfort in the stillness. She hadn't meant to fall asleep, but exhaustion had won.

A sharp jerk beneath her fingertips startled her awake.

Nevell's body spasmed violently, his limbs thrashing against the bed. Panic gripped Simetra as she sprang upright. "Help me! Somebody, please help me!" Her voice was raw, desperate.

The door burst open, and a male nurse rushed in. He peeled Nevell's trembling fingers free from Simetra's grasp, his movements swift and practiced. Without hesitation, he yanked the call light and shouted into the intercom, "I need help in here, stat!"

Simetra pressed a hand to her mouth, willing herself to stay strong. "Hold on, Nevell. I'm right here. I'm right here."

The nurse turned to her, his expression firm but not unkind. "Miss, I need you to step out."

Simetra shook her head violently. "I'm not going anywhere. He needs to know that I got him."

The nurse didn't argue. He simply moved; his grip unyielding as he ushered her toward the door. Simetra fought against it, but he was stronger, and she was losing the battle.

The door closed between them, sealing Nevell inside with the chaos—and leaving Simetra on the outside, helpless.

Outside in the hallway, Dr. Rossmore stood beside Simetra, who leaned against the wall, exhaustion pressing down on her like a weight she couldn't shake.

"Ms. Thomas, you really need to go home and get some rest," he said gently. "You've been here all night. Mr. Carter is holding his own. You won't be any good to him if you get sick."

Simetra barely registered the words. Her mind was stuck in the moment she'd seen Nevell convulsing, his body betraying him in ways she didn't understand. She swallowed hard. "Can you at least tell me what happened to Nevell?"

Dr. Rossmore sighed, his tone measured but grave. "We're not sure what caused Mr. Carter's seizure. We ran a CT scan and an MRI, and we discovered a small brain bleed."

Simetra stiffened. "What does that mean?"

"Blood is pooling in his brain," he explained. "If we don't stop the bleeding, he could suffer a stroke—or worse."

A sharp pain twisted in Simetra's chest, and she clutched at it instinctively, forcing herself to take a deep breath. Worse. She didn't even want to consider what that meant.

Dr. Rossmore's voice remained calm, but there was urgency beneath it. "I can stop the bleeding, but it requires surgery."

"So what are you waiting for?" Simetra's voice came out harsher than she intended, raw with fear.

Dr. Rossmore hesitated. "Mr. Carter doesn't have a living will in place, and in his current condition, he can't sign the consent form.

Without a power of attorney or legal guardianship—"

"I'll get the guardianship." The words tumbled out before she could even think them through. A part of her was still stunned that she was saying them at all. But there was no other choice. "I can't believe I even have to say this, but please—please save my brother."

Dr. Rossmore gave her a reassuring nod. "I'll do what I can, Ms. Thomas."

Dr. Rossmore handed Simetra a clipboard and a pen, his expression unreadable, but the weight of the moment was crushing her. Her fingers trembled as she took them, staring down at the crisp forms that held Nevell's fate in sterile, black ink.

She swallowed hard. No turning back now.

With a deep breath, she scrawled her signature in the designated spaces, each stroke feeling heavier than the last. When she finished, the doctor took the clipboard and left her alone with her brother.

Simetra sank into the chair beside Nevell's bed and reached for his hand, wrapping her fingers around his motionless ones. The

steady hum of machines surrounded them—
blinking monitors, a quiet beeping, the soft
whoosh of the ventilator that was keeping
him alive.

Her gaze drifted over him, taking in the way
the tubes and wires connected him to the
medical world, keeping him suspended in
this fragile state. A medically induced
coma—his body's way of surviving the
trauma. But it didn't look like survival. It
looked like something far too close to the
edge.

She exhaled shakily and squeezed his hand.
"I got you, Nevell. I swear I do."

But as she sat in the stillness, watching his
chest rise and fall only because of the
machine, she wondered if she was already
too late.

CHAPTER 22

Morning light filtered through the glass walls, casting a soft glow over Nevell's indoor pool. Simetra stood at the edge, barefoot, her arms wrapped around herself despite the warmth in the air.

Without hesitation, she jumped.

The water swallowed her whole. She sank quickly, her body descending to the deep end like a stone. She didn't fight it. She didn't kick. She just let herself drop until her feet met the bottom.

Time stretched. Seconds bled into minutes.

She kept her eyes closed, her lungs burning, her body screaming at her to rise—but she resisted. She stayed beneath the surface, floating in the silence, in the weightlessness.

Finally, the ache in her chest became unbearable. She pushed herself upward, slicing through the water, reaching for air.

She surfaced with a violent gasp, sucking in breath so deep it hurt.

And then she screamed. A raw, guttural sound that ripped from her throat and echoed through the room, bouncing off the walls, swallowed only by the stillness of the water around her.

Simetra climbed out of the pool. Her mind drifting, Nevell lying motionless in the hospital bed, his face pale against the harsh white sheets. Tubes snaked around him, machines whispered in the background, sustaining him in ways she never imagined he would need.

This wasn't the brother she knew.

Her mind drifted back to elementary school, to the moment she first understood what it meant to have someone truly fight for her.

She had been small—smaller than most of the kids in her grade. And the boy who chased her was older, bigger, reckless in the way kids often are when they don't know how to handle their emotions. He had liked her, apparently, but in the worst way— pulling at her backpack, dragging her to the ground like she was some prize he could take.

Nevell had been older.

And he hadn't hesitated.

He found them just as Simetra had hit the dirt, her palms scraped raw, her chest tight with fear. The boy hadn't expected the fury in Nevell's stance, the sharpness in his voice as he yanked him back and made him understand—very clearly—that Simetra was not someone to be bullied, chased, or taken advantage of.

After that day, no one at school dared to push her around. Not when they knew who her big brother was.

Simetra toweled dry, closely examining her arms and legs. She couldn't help but think about Nevell in his sterile room; she could hardly believe that same fierce protector was the fragile man hanging on to life.

A shell of his former self.

Simetra's chest heaved, her breath coming in sharp, uneven gasps.

A sob tore from her throat.

"What if I can never get you back?" she choked out, her voice fractured, barely above a whisper. "What am I going to do?"

The answer to her agonizing question was met with silence that felt like it was swallowing her whole.

CHAPTER 23

Simetra shifted in the leather chair, the polished surface creaking beneath her as she folded her hands in her lap. Across from her, **Damon O'Neal**—Nevell's lawyer—studied her with a measured gaze, his fingers tapping against the thick stack of notebooks before sliding them across the desk toward her.

She hesitated, staring at the weight of responsibility in front of her. "What are these?" she asked, lifting the first notebook, its worn edges suggesting years of meticulous record-keeping.

"Homework," Damon replied simply, leaning back in his chair as if gauging her reaction.

Simetra scoffed, arching an eyebrow. "What kind of homework?" She balanced the files precariously, flipping open the top one. Pages lined with figures and terms she barely understood stared back at her.

Damon sighed, rubbing his temples. "This is information about Nevell's accounts. The anniversary of several of his contracts is in ten days."

Simetra blinked at him. "You want me to memorize all this stuff?"

"Not memorize, but at least familiarize yourself with them." He folded his hands over the desk, his tone patient but firm. "You need to look over the current allocations. As a shareholder, you need to know as much as you can about the contracts."

She shook her head, shutting the notebook with a dull thud. "Wait a minute. You're moving too fast. Besides, the broker said he would handle all that."

Damon's jaw tightened. "You don't have a clue how serious this is, do you?" He leaned forward, the weight of his words pressing against the cool air between them. "I must warn you, your actions regarding your brother's accounts from this day forward will either get you an 'atta girl' or a cot in a prison cell."

A chill ran down Simetra's spine. "What is that supposed to mean?" she asked, flipping through the pages absently, as if the answers would materialize before her.

Damon's gaze darkened. "It means you can't buy yourself a new car or get your nails done with Nevell's money." His tone was sharp, slicing through the office's silence. "It's called misappropriation of funds, and if a judge decides to come after you for abuse, it could land you in serious legal trouble."

Simetra swallowed, her fingers gripping the edge of the notebook. "I would never take advantage of Nevell's money."

Damon exhaled slowly, tapping a finger against the desk. "I'm not the one you need to convince."

The office was quiet, save for the rhythmic ticking of a clock somewhere in the shadows. Time passed slowly after Simetra left. Damon O'Neal stood before the heavy steel safe embedded in the mahogany-paneled wall, keying in the combination with slow precision. The latch clicked, and he pulled the door open, revealing neatly stacked legal documents, bound contracts, and, at the forefront, Nevell's will.

Damon exhaled, lifting the thick envelope with practiced care before settling back into his chair. As he flipped through the pages, reading the legal jargon with the scrutiny of a seasoned lawyer, a knock at the door interrupted him.

Roderic Sherman, a law clerk, arrived at Damon O'Neal's office, fresh from the courthouse. He held the permanent letters of guardianship for Simetra.

"I can't believe how fast these came through," Roderic said, setting them down. "The temporary letters were just signed."

Damon barely looked up, absorbed in Nevell Carter's will. He exhaled through his nose. "Ms. Thomas is in over her head."

Roderic glanced at the thick stack of papers on Damon's desk. "I hope things work out for them. Carter's estate is massive—I respect her for wanting to handle it herself."

Damon's expression remained unreadable. "I just hope she's as honest as she seems."

"You think she's in it for the money?" Roderic asked, raising a brow.

Damon leaned back, tapping a finger against the arm of his chair. "That remains to be seen."

Roderic gave a wry smile. "It wouldn't be unreasonable for her to benefit from Carter's wealth while he's still alive."

Damon slid the will across the desk. "Take a look for yourself. You'll find it quite interesting."

CHAPTER 24

Levi exhaled sharply as he settled into the driver's seat, the weight of the day pressing down on his shoulders like a fifty-pound weight. He glimpsed the precinct doors swing closed behind him in the rearview mirror as he pulled onto the street, the hum of traffic blending with his own thoughts.

The case wasn't adding up. He couldn't put his hand on exactly what, but something about it gnawed at him. It was like an itch just out of reach.

His phone buzzed against the dashboard, the sharp vibration cutting through his haze. He snatched it up.

"Levi."

Greg Shepherd's voice came through tense, clipped. "Just got the forensics report back."

Levi straightened in his seat, weaving through the slow-moving cars ahead.

"Find anything?"

A pause. "No prints. No DNA. Clean as a damn whistle."

Levi's fingers tightened around the wheel. "Figures."

"But—" Shepherd's tone shifted, a thread of urgency. "Someone recognized the machine in the burned-out photo. Said there's another one just like it sitting in a warehouse in Norfolk."

Levi's pulse quickened. A lead. A real one.

"Thought you might want to take a look," Shepherd added.

Levi's foot pressed down, edging the accelerator forward. Anticipation made his stomach lurch.

Ahead, the traffic on the James River Bridge had ground to a halt.

He clenched his jaw, drumming his fingers against the steering wheel. The timing was perfect for the bridge to be jammed. Norfolk was waiting on the other side. The machine, the case, the answers, it was all hanging just out of reach.

And Levi hated waiting.

He continued to drum his fingers against the steering wheel, watching the endless line of brake lights stretching across the James

River Bridge. The traffic wasn't moving. It hadn't moved for the last ten minutes. A familiar ringtone cut through the idle silence. He glanced at the screen on his cell phone, then tapped the answer button.

"Hey, George. What's up?" Levi asked, adjusting in his seat.

George's voice carried an unusual urgency. "I just saw something you might think is important."

Levi sighed, staring at the stagnant sea of cars ahead. "Right now, I'm in stop-and-go traffic. Might as well talk to you face-to-face." He opened his phone, switching to FaceTime.

George's face appeared on the screen; his brow furrowed as he glanced at the monitor beside him. "I'm looking at my security cameras now. A van from Shady Crest Funeral Home just picked up a body that's been in the morgue for at least two weeks."

Levi frowned. "So? Is that a bad thing?"

"Nah, man," George said, shaking his head. "But a family member has to claim the body before we can release it to a funeral home.

Nobody had asked about this guy until today."

Levi's grip tightened around his phone. "How do you know all this?"

George hesitated. "I ain't supposed to be talking about it, but... The guy got electrocuted, and nobody said a word about it. I've been keeping my eyes and ears open in case someone from the man's family came looking for him. But instead of a family member showing up, they're shipping him off to Shady Crest right now."

Levi felt the air around him grow heavier. He narrowed his eyes. "Would the guy's name happen to be Spencer Walach?"

George blinked in surprise. "Why, yeah. How'd you know?"

Levi didn't answer. The adrenaline hit fast. He cut the call, tossed his phone onto the passenger seat, and flipped on his lights and siren. The traffic wouldn't budge—but that didn't mean he couldn't carve his own path.

With a sharp turn of the wheel, he maneuvered through the sluggish chaos ahead.

"I've got to get a hold of that body."

Levi pushed through the double doors of Shady Crest Funeral Home, the sharp scent of disinfectant mixing with the faint perfume of lilies. His badge glinted under the fluorescent lighting as he raised it in front of the funeral director.

"I'm looking for the body of Spencer Walach," he said, his voice firm.

Toby Bass, a man in his late fifties with thinning hair and an air of indifference, barely looked up from his clipboard. "I'm sorry, but Mr. Walach's remains are already in the retort. And it's up and running."

Levi felt his pulse spike. His jaw tightened. "Well, shut it down!" he barked. "I need you to stop the process right now."

Toby sighed heavily, as if Levi had just disrupted his evening plans. He turned toward the antique phone mounted on the wall, lifted the receiver, and punched in a number with slow deliberation.

"Shut down the retort," he said into the receiver, his voice flat. A pause. He exhaled. "Yeah, I know. Just do it."

Levi crossed his arms. "I'll take the remains of the remains in a bag to go."

Toby snorted. "Ha! Ha! Very funny."

Levi didn't blink. "You don't see me laughing."

Toby finally set the phone down, regarding Levi with weary curiosity. "So, I guess we're not getting paid for the pickup now?"

Levi's lips curled into a humorless smirk. "To the contrary, Toby. I'm going to make sure you get paid." His voice dropped, the tension thick in the room. "You see, it looks like we've got ourselves a crime here."

The air between them shifted. It hung heavy, filled with uncertainty. Toby's grip on his clipboard tightened just slightly.

Levi had seen that look before. It meant something wasn't right.

CHAPTER 25

Levi loomed over Scott Colton, his presence weighted with frustration. Scott sat stiffly at his desk, his expression composed but wary. The air between them crackled with unspoken tension.

"I'm in a pretty bad position right now, Mr. Colton," Levi said, his voice measured yet firm. "I wish I could impress upon you the gravity of the situation."

With a practiced motion, Levi opened a file and placed it in front of Scott. The detective's gaze didn't waver as he studied the hospital administrator, waiting for a response.

Scott exhaled slowly, adjusting his posture. "Detective Stone, I've told you before—I'm more than willing to help. My offer still stands. But what you're asking…" He shook his head. "It's impossible without a warrant."

Levi arched an eyebrow. "Unless I'm mistaken, the hospital should be filing a complaint on Mr. Walach's behalf." He paused, letting the weight of his words settle before leaning in slightly. A note of sarcasm crept into his tone. "Oh, wait—you can't file a complaint, can you? Because you signed the release of the body to the funeral home."

Scott stiffened. "I did no such thing."

Without hesitation, Levi flipped a page in the file and pointed to a signature. "This is yours, isn't it?"

Scott's eyes narrowed as he examined the signature. "It certainly is not."

Levi's gaze burned into him. "Then why would someone forge it?"

"That's what I intend to find out."

Levi wasn't satisfied. His patience had worn thin. "I need to speak with everyone who had contact with Mr. Walach while he was at Mercy."

Scott met Levi's stare, his voice unwavering. "Detective, that is also impossible."

Levi leaned in, his proximity meant to intimidate. "Then find a way to make it possible. Because if you don't, I'll arrest you for disposing of a body that was evidence in a police investigation."

Scott didn't flinch. He simply tilted his head, considering Levi's words with the detached confidence of a man who had already measured the risks. "If you truly believed that, you wouldn't be threatening me." He leaned back, exhaling sharply. "The way I see it, there's no complaint, and there's no body. Therefore, there's no crime—just an unfortunate accident."

Silence stretched between them before Scott delivered his final blow. "Just so we're clear, the hospital had to send Mr. Walach out to be cremated. He wasn't embalmed, and his condition deteriorated rapidly."

Scott pushed his chair back and stood, stepping deliberately into Levi's space. The detective held firm, but Scott's intent was clear. He was dismissing him.

"If there's nothing else, Detective," Scott said, motioning toward the door, "I have work to do."

Levi's jaw tightened, but he said nothing. With one last glance at the file on the desk, he turned to walk out.

Scott Colton leaned back in his chair, his expression composed but firm. "Detective, if you come back with a warrant, you'll be wasting your time. Every employee has signed non-disclosure waivers. They won't talk to you."

Levi's lips curled into a tight smirk. "How convenient."

He took a slow step forward, eyes locked on Scott like a predator sizing up its prey. "You're hiding something, and I'm going to find it."

Scott didn't flinch. He merely inclined his head, his voice carrying a note of finality. "I wish you the best, Detective."

Levi held his gaze for a beat longer, searching for even the faintest flicker of hesitation in Colton's demeanor. He found none. With a sharp turn, he pivoted on his heel and strode out the door.

Scott didn't move. Didn't call after him. He simply watched as Levi disappeared down the hallway, his expression unreadable.

But as the door clicked shut, a slow exhale escaped Scott's lips. Whatever Levi thought he was onto—it was going to take more than determination to crack it open.

CHAPTER 26

Nevell's study was steeped in quiet opulence—walls adorned with expensive paintings, a towering bookshelf lined with meticulously arranged volumes. Simetra and Phyllis stepped inside, their eyes sweeping across the space.

"It feels weird in here without Nevell behind his desk," Simetra murmured, the absence of her brother a tangible weight.

Phyllis nodded, trailing her fingers along the smooth leather of an armchair. "I can see him here. All this leather, all manly."

Simetra's gaze settled on one of the paintings. She hesitated for only a moment before reaching up, pulling it from the wall to reveal the safe hidden behind it. Without a word, she keyed in the code, and the mechanism clicked open. Her breath hitched as she pulled out several thick bundles of cash. The sight of it alone felt unreal. She held up the money, her hands shaking slightly.

"Can you believe this? I'm really in over my head."

Phyllis stared at the stacks of bills, wide-eyed. "This is crazy. I didn't know Nevell had it like this."

"He still has it." Simetra's voice was quiet but firm. "This is all still Nevell's. I'm just taking care of it until he gets better."

Phyllis glanced at her, measuring the weight of those words. "What if that doesn't happen?"

"I don't even want to think like that." Simetra swallowed hard. "I'm still trying to wrap my head around him being hurt."

Phyllis folded her arms, her expression unreadable. "Well, he is hurt, and you're going to have to deal with it. Technically, he belongs to you now." She gestured around the lavish office. "So, all this belongs to you. Just remember what they say about money changing people... and this kind of money? A definite changer."

Simetra hesitated, then carefully returned the money to the safe. She closed it with deliberate precision, sealing it behind the painting once more.

"I don't care about the money," she said, her voice thick with emotion. "I just want my brother back."

Phyllis sighed. "I hate to be the harbinger of doom, but you may not be able to fix Nevell."

Simetra shook her head. "I have to try. He's the only blood relative I have left." Her gaze flickered across the room, taking in the wealth, the grandeur—everything Nevell had surrounded himself with. "Somewhere along the way, he got caught up in the value of all this stuff."

A long silence stretched between them, heavy and unresolved.

Simetra sighed, running a hand along the edge of Nevell's desk. "Sometimes it feels like he lost the value of our kinship," she murmured. "But I understand the value of blood, and that's always been more important to me than money."

Phyllis watched her carefully. "If I were you, I wouldn't even think about going back to work."

Simetra shook her head. "I have to go back. I'd go crazy if I had to sit around, watching Nevell sleep all day and night."

She turned to the computer on his desk, opening it with a few taps of the keyboard. Files lined the screen, but some were locked behind layers of encryption. Simetra exhaled sharply, frustration bubbling beneath her calm exterior.

"I found some files I can't access," she muttered. "I need you to use your hacking skills and help me find out what Nevell's keeping secret."

Phyllis smirked, resting a hand on her hip. "Doll, I'm sure we aren't even gonna scratch the surface of what Nevell is hiding."

Simetra leaned in. "Nevell's lawyer made it his business to go into the safe before I did. He was adamant that I not see Nevell's will. I was hoping something on his computer might be helpful."

Phyllis rubbed her fingers together, excitement lighting her eyes. "Now you've got me curious. Shall we?"

With a practiced ease, Phyllis started bypassing Nevell's firewalls, her fingers flying over the keyboard. Simetra perched herself on the edge of the desk, watching her work.

Moments later, Phyllis let out a triumphant laugh. "Get over here, Doll. I'm in. What do you wanna look into first?"

Simetra leaned over Phyllis' shoulder as she opened an encrypted file. Lists of medical supply companies scrolled down the screen—Midtown Medical Supply, Vista Medical, MedSouth.

Simetra's eyes widened. "Hold up. These names sound familiar. I've seen them before."

Phyllis cocked her head. "Maybe when you were preparing the billing for your patients?"

"No, that's not it." Simetra's brow furrowed. "I got a list of these same companies from Nevell's lawyer."

Phyllis exhaled sharply, sitting back in her chair. A slow smirk curved her lips. "Well, shut my mouth."

Phyllis' phone buzzed sharply, slicing through the stillness of the room. She answered on the first ring, her tone clipped.

"Can I call you back? I'm in the middle of something important."

She pushed up from Nevell's desk, turning her back to Simetra as she lowered her voice.

"Yes. I understand… I'm not sure how long that could take."

Simetra watched as Phyllis listened intently, her posture rigid, brows furrowed. Whoever was on the other end had her full attention, but their words remained just beyond reach.

Phyllis sighed, impatience edging her voice. "Keep your choners on. I'm on my way."

She disconnected the call with a sharp press of her thumb.

Simetra stood, folding her arms. "What gives?"

"I've got to track down some missing equipment."

Simetra glanced at the clock. "Doesn't whoever that was know it's the middle of the night?"

Phyllis flashed a dry smile, raising both hands to make air quotes. "I'm on call. One of the perks of being 'The Maintenance Supervisor.'"

Simetra frowned. "This can't wait until morning?"

Phyllis hesitated for just a fraction of a second. "That was Scott Colton on the phone. It's the damndest thing—the electroshock machine that fried the homeless guy is missing."

Simetra's breath hitched. "What did you just say?"

"I have to find a machine involved in an accident that resulted in a fatality," Phyllis muttered, rubbing her temples. "Like I can just pull it out of my ass."

She grabbed her bag and moved toward the door. Simetra wasn't about to let her go alone.

"Wait for me," she said, falling into step beside her. "I'm coming with."

CHAPTER 27

The hospital maintenance storage room was vast, dimly lit, and crammed with forgotten equipment. Rows upon rows of boxes, crates, and bins lined the space, filled with outdated machinery no longer in use. The air carried a faint scent of dust and metal, heavy with disuse.

Simetra and Phyllis moved cautiously through the maze of discarded tools and devices, their footsteps echoing against the cold tile floor. At the end of a row, a large cabinet jutted out, its presence unnatural, as though it had been placed there in haste.

Without hesitation, Simetra pulled open the door. The shelves inside were packed with broken-down electroshock and breathing machines, their worn-out frames stacked haphazardly. She lifted her phone, angling the lens to record the scene.

"I've seen so many serial numbers my eyes are running together," she muttered, frustration seeping into her voice. "This way, you can double-check later to make sure you got the right machine."

Phyllis exhaled, rubbing a hand over her face. "Thanks, Doll. We've gotta find it. Not finding that machine is the kind of shit that'll get me canned."

Simetra glanced down at her phone, her eyes narrowing at the time displayed on the screen. "Scott wouldn't go that far," she said, disbelief laced in her words.

Phyllis scoffed. "He's the guy who sends other people to do his dirty work. How do you think I got promoted to this job?"

Simetra turned to her, curiosity flickering in her gaze. "What do you mean?"

Phyllis shook her head, a smirk tugging at the corner of her mouth. "Trust me, you don't want to know."

Simetra hesitated but chose not to press further.

Phyllis straightened, glancing around the cramped space. "Come on," she said, her tone crisp with determination. "We've got some other places to look."

The door marked *SCRAP* swung open, and Phyllis flicked on the overhead light. The dull fluorescent light buzzed to life, casting uneven shadows across the cavernous space.

Piles of discarded equipment lay in tangled heaps, broken machines sprawled across the floor like remnants of forgotten experiments.

Simetra stepped inside, surveying the wreckage. "From the looks of this place, if it's here, it's already dismantled."

Phyllis strode forward, pulling back a sliding door that revealed an open incinerator. The sight of it made her grimace.

"Not just dismantled, Doll. If it made it this far, it's history."

Simetra glanced around uneasily. "How much more ground do we have to cover?"

"We haven't checked *The Outback* yet," Phyllis said, nodding toward the rear of the building. "That's where they dump equipment set to be sold off or refurbished."

Simetra sighed, checking the time on her phone. "Alright, but it's way late. I have to get up in the morning."

Phyllis considered her for a moment, then lifted a brow. "Why don't we split up? You search here, and I'll check *The Outback*. I know the place—it's creepy, but I'm used to it."

Simetra hesitated, then nodded. "Fine. Just—be careful."

Phyllis smirked. "Always am."

She turned and disappeared into the dim corridors, leaving Simetra alone with the mountains of scrap.

Simetra moved cautiously, rifling through crates of discarded parts. Metal clinked beneath her fingers as she sifted through broken components, searching for anything resembling the missing electroshock machine. She was so focused that it took her a moment to register the sound—a faint but deliberate rhythm.

Footsteps.

She froze.

They weren't Phyllis'. These steps were slow, methodical, coming from the entrance of the storage area.

Her breath hitched.

Someone was here.

Simetra sprinted back toward the SCRAP room, her pulse hammering in her ears.

Behind her, the footsteps quickened, mirroring her own frantic pace.

She barely registered the sliding door as she tore past it, bursting into the incinerator room. Her breath came in sharp gasps— panic clawing at her throat. With nowhere else to go, she scrambled inside the incinerator, wedging herself against the wall beside the furnace.

Through the narrow gap, she saw a tall shadow stretching across the floor.

The man moved deliberately, his gait steady, his destination clear.

Straight for her.

Simetra squeezed her eyes shut, pressing both hands over her mouth to stifle the sound of her breath. Just beyond the door, she heard him pause. The silence was worse than the footsteps. There was an unbearable moment stretched tight with anticipation.

Then there was movement.

The incinerator door swung shut with a heavy clang. A sickening finality echoed in the small space, followed by the unmistakable click of the lock.

Trapped.

Simetra's panic erupted in full force. She pushed against the door, hands scrambling over the smooth metal, but it wouldn't budge. Her breath came too fast, too shallow. Darkness pressed in from all sides. A rush of dizziness blurred her vision, and her limbs grew heavy.

Somewhere in the distance, footsteps receded. The man was leaving.

Simetra's knees buckled, and she slid down the wall.

Hands caught her.

"Jesus, Doll!" Phyllis' voice was sharp with shock. "How the hell did you lock yourself in here?"

Simetra sucked in ragged breaths, struggling to regain control. "I didn't," she managed, her voice weak. "Someone else did."

Phyllis' expression darkened. She spun, scanning the space behind her, but the shadowy corridor was empty.

She pulled Simetra to her feet. "Come on, let's get you out of here."

CHAPTER 28

Days had passed, but the alley behind Mercy Hospital remained as grim and forgotten as ever. Cecil crouched in the narrow gap between the loading dock and the building, the stench of rot and damp concrete thick in the air.

His fingers sifted through piles of discarded trash—plastic wrappers, crushed cans, torn bits of newspaper that fluttered weakly as he pushed them aside. His search was methodical, almost desperate, until his hand brushed against something beneath a heap of rags.

A bag.

Black leather, zipped tightly at the top.

His pulse kicked up as he pulled it free, wiping grime off its surface before cautiously unzipping it.

The sight inside made his stomach twist.

Cecil slammed the bag shut, breath hitching as he glanced around, his eyes darting through the shadows for any sign of movement. The alley was silent—just the soft rustle of the wind through scattered debris. Still, the feeling that someone could be watching gnawed at him.

Instinctively, he clutched the bag tighter against his chest.

He wasn't leaving what was inside behind.

Cecil hesitated, gripping the worn leather bag. Ole Spence would never have given it up willingly.

Glancing over his shoulder, he checked for onlookers before carefully tipping the bag open. The contents tumbled out—familiar fragments of Spencer Walach's life. As Cecil thumbed through the items, memories surfaced, taking him back to the gas station where they first met.

He had been lingering too long, and the attendant didn't take kindly to loiterers. The man had come at Cecil with a club, eyes burning with disdain. Before the first swing could land, Spencer stepped in, gripping Cecil's arm and hauling him to safety.

From that day on, Ole Spence had taken him under his wing. He showed him how to get by and where to find scraps of cover to ward off the cold. Under Spencer's tutelage, Cecil learned how to panhandle for enough to eat.

Now, staring at the contents of the old bag, Cecil wondered how a man like Spence could ever let it go.

Cecil froze. He thought he heard soft footsteps, maybe the scrape of a boot against pavement. His pulse quickened as he scanned the alley, but all he saw was shifting darkness. A shadow moved—he swore it did.

He shoved Spencer's stash back into the bag, fingers fumbling as unease crept up his spine. Someone was watching him. He could feel it, a cold, calculating presence lurking just beyond his sight.

One last glance around confirmed what he already knew. This place wasn't safe anymore. And where the hell was Ole Spence? He hadn't been back in over a week. Cecil didn't like that. Not one bit.

He needed to find a new spot to sleep tonight. The usual chaos in the alley. The trucks unloading at the hospital. The distant chatter had always been comforting. But now? Now it felt off.

And Mama Simetra, she hadn't come by with food lately. That was strange, too.

Something was wrong.

Cecil bolted from the alley, his heart hammering in his chest. He didn't stop— didn't dare look back.

Minutes later, a tall figure emerged from the shadows. A ball cap hid his face, a black mask obscuring everything but his eyes.

He moved slowly, deliberately, scanning the ground. Then he spotted a slip of paper, carelessly dropped in Cecil's haste.

Stooping down, he picked it up, turning it over in his gloved fingers before slipping it into his pocket, then melted back into the darkness.

CHAPTER 29

Simetra sat at Nevell's desk, the weight of responsibility pressing down on her. A stack of his notebooks lay beside her, filled with careful calculations and scribbled thoughts she hadn't yet had the courage to read. The glow of her laptop screen illuminated the study, casting long shadows as she stared at Damon O'Neal's face on the Zoom call. His expression was steady, professional—too detached for her liking.

"You need to sell the stock, Simetra," Damon said, his voice crisp, measured. "The courts will allow you to liquidate Nevell's assets for his care."

Simetra blinked, barely believing the words. "He doesn't need the money."

Damon's jaw tightened. "You don't know that. You don't know how long he'll be incapacitated—it could be years."

Her stomach twisted at the thought. "God wouldn't do that to me."

He sighed, leaning forward slightly. "I know you have faith. But faith alone isn't enough. Nevell's injuries—" He hesitated, choosing his words carefully. "You have to prepare for the possibility that he may never fully recover."

Simetra sat straighter, defiant. "Nevell is strong. He survived the crash. He's going to walk out of that hospital on his own two feet."

Damon studied her, his gaze unwavering. "I wish I had your confidence," he said quietly. "But you need to think about long-term care. The courts will support whatever decision you make."

Simetra shook her head. "I will never put Nevell in a nursing home."

"Never say never." Damon exhaled, rubbing his forehead as if weighing how much more to push. Then he reached for a folder on his desk, holding it up to the camera. "I've sent you plenty of reading material. One of my paralegals will drop off the paperwork at your home."

She swallowed hard, pushing down the dread pooling in her chest. "Thanks for everything, Damon."

His expression softened just a fraction. "If you need me, I'm just a phone call away."

As the call ended, the screen dimmed, leaving her alone in the quiet study. Simetra glanced at the stack of notebooks again, the weight of uncertainty settling deep in her bones.

Everything was coming at her too fast.

Nevell's investments needed attention—his condition was stable, but the outlook was grim. And on top of it all, she was no closer to unraveling why Scott Colton was so intent on burying the truth about Spencer Walach.

She exhaled sharply and told Alexa to play something soft. The gentle hum of piano notes filled the room, wrapping around her like a fragile barrier against the chaos pressing in.

Closing her eyes, she massaged her temples, willing the tension in her body to ease.

She leaned back, trying to let herself sink into the moment—just one moment of calm.

But she wasn't alone.

The camera perched on the bookshelf stood watch, its unblinking lens capturing her every move.

CHAPTER 30

Evening had settled in, casting long shadows across Levi's desk. He sat hunched over a manila folder, fingers tracing the worn edges as he pulled out a photograph.

The image was unsettling, a burned machine, charred and lifeless, frozen in time.

He turned it over.

Bold, hurried handwriting scrawled across the back:

MEET ME ACROSS FROM THE LOADING DOCK BEHIND MERCY HOSPITAL AT 9:00 PM TONIGHT. IT'S IMPORTANT.

Levi frowned, reading it twice. The message carried urgency, maybe even desperation.

It's 8:30 p.m. outside the loading dock at Mercy Hospital. The air smelled of motor oil and damp pavement. Workers moved in and out of the loading bay, their chatter blending with the hum of idling trucks. Levi kept his distance, his car parked just beyond the reach of the floodlights. The slip of paper burned in his hand.

MEET ME ACROSS FROM THE LOADING DOCK BEHIND MERCY HOSPITAL AT 9:00 PM TONIGHT. IT'S IMPORTANT.

He stared at the hospital's back entrance, scanning the shadows. Who had sent this? And why did they want to meet in person?

A confession? A warning? Or something worse?

Levi glanced at his watch—8:35 PM. Still time to leave.

His gut told him this wasn't going to be simple.

He exhaled slowly. Whatever was about to happen, it felt less like a meeting and more like a reckoning.

Levi cut the engine in his car, his fingers drumming lightly against the steering wheel. The alley was alive in its own way, with shadows moving, voices murmuring, and the occasional scrape of a shopping cart against the concrete.

Homeless people lay curled up along the walls, some in restless sleep, others watching with wary eyes. A man pushing a battered shopping cart slowed as he neared Levi's car. Then, deliberately, he stepped closer and knocked on the window.

Levi sighed, rolling it down just enough to be heard.

"Get out of here if you don't want to spend the night in county lockup."

The man didn't flinch. Instead, he leaned his back against the car, studying Levi as if he had expected resistance.

"I'm Justin Ambrose."

Levi narrowed his eyes. "Should I know you?"

"I'm the person who sent you the picture of Spencer Walach." Justin's voice was steady but carried an edge. "I was one of the nurses assisting with Mr. Walach's shock treatment. Heard you've been asking questions about what happened the day he died."

Levi hesitated for a beat before pushing open the car door and stepping out. The air was damp, the sounds of the loading dock filtered through from the street beyond.

"I need you to tell me everything," Levi said. "From the beginning."

Justin shook his head. "I don't have time for all that." He reached into his coat, pulling something from the folds of worn fabric. "I came here to bring you something you need to see."

Across the alley, a second truck rumbled toward the loading bay, its headlights cutting through the dim evening haze. The first truck pulled out too fast, nearly sideswiping the incoming vehicle. Horns blared. Drivers threw their fists in frustration, shouting over the screech of brakes.

Levi barely glanced at the commotion. His focus was on the narrow gap between the wall and the adjacent building—an alcove cloaked in shadow.

Justin stood beside him, gripping the edge of his shopping cart. Levi peered inside the darkness, searching for movement.

Justin exhaled sharply. "I snuck it out of the maintenance scrap room."

Levi straightened, his gaze narrowing. "What is it?"

Justin pulled the tarp away, revealing a machine burned beyond recognition. The charred metal had soot staining every surface. The scent of ashes still clung to it.

"The electroshock machine used on Mr. Walach that day."

Levi took an involuntary step closer, his breath catching at the sight.

"It wasn't easy," Justin continued, voice thick with something heavier than guilt. "But I had to do something. I lost my job because of that accident. A man lost his life. Somebody other than me and Carla needs to be held accountable." He glanced at the ruined device. "I hope this can raise some questions. Get some answers."

Levi pulled out his phone, snapping photos, fingers steady despite the pulse pounding in his ears. "I need my own copy of the evidence."

A sudden screech shattered the moment.

Both men turned just as the back of a truck barreled toward them, reversing too fast, too recklessly.

Levi lunged out of the way, but his foot caught on uneven pavement.

He stumbled backward, falling hard and plunging straight into the darkness between the buildings.

Justin was right on Levi's heels. He ended up being too close, too slow.

The truck roared backward, tires shrieking against the pavement.

Metal crunched. The shopping cart crumpled like paper, and the electroshock machine—Justin's last piece of evidence—vanished beneath the wheels, shattered beyond recognition.

Then the truck stopped.

Levi turned just in time to see Justin pinned against the cold brick wall, his body crushed, unmoving.

"No."

Levi ran to him, heart pounding, hands shaking as he reached out. Blood trickled from Justin's nose and mouth, pooling in the deep creases of his face.

He pressed two fingers to Justin's neck. Nothing.

"No. No. No."

His breath came in short gasps. The weight of it all—the destroyed evidence, the senseless death pressed down on him, crushing as surely as the truck had crushed Justin.

Levi squeezed his eyes shut, his knees hitting the pavement.

Justin Ambrose was gone.

CHAPTER 31

The office was quiet, the soft hum of the computer the only sound as Simetra sifted through paperwork at her desk. The fluorescent lights overhead cast a pale glow across the polished surface.

The door creaked open, and Ray Stewart stepped inside, his expression stiff with concern. He clutched a copy of his medical bill in one hand and eased into the chair across from her.

"Ma'am, I'm Ray Stewart," he said, shifting the paper between his fingers. "I was looking over my bill and noticed some charges for my newest prosthesis. Can you give me a rundown of what I'm actually being charged for?"

Simetra took the bill, scanning the list of expenses with a practiced eye. "It looks like there's a charge for the upgrade and another one for maintenance." She frowned. "The maintenance fee is already included in the cost of the upgrade, so that shouldn't be a separate charge. And these other charges—" she tapped the paper "—they look like duplicates."

Ray exhaled sharply, shaking his head. "What do you want me to do while I wait for the corrected bill? I don't want this messing with my credit because I didn't pay on time."

Simetra set the paper down, her brows drawing together in a frown. "I can contact your insurance provider and get them to generate a new bill, hopefully reversing the duplicate charges."

Ray let out a low chuckle—one that held no amusement. "I wouldn't even have looked at the bill if my insurance hadn't told me they weren't going to cover it."

His jaw tightened, frustration simmering just beneath his words. Simetra folded her hands on the desk, meeting his gaze.

"I'll do what I can to fix this, Mr. Stewart."

Simetra sat forward slightly, studying the man across from her. Ray Stewart was built like someone who had endured hard labor, but the missing arm and the way he absently rubbed his chest spoke of battles lost.

"If you don't mind me asking," she said, "how did you lose your arm?"

Ray let out a short chuckle—gruff, self-deprecating. "I'm an electrician. A pretty dumb one, apparently." He leaned back, shaking his head. "I was installing a conveyor in a warehouse. Thought I turned off the power. Guess I didn't—because when I grabbed the wire, it was hot." His voice was steady, matter-of-fact, but the weight of the memory lingered. "Got electrocuted."

Simetra winced. "I'm really sorry."

Ray waved it off, tapping a hand against his chest. "Messed up my heart, too. Got this handy-dandy defibrillator in here now."

Simetra's gaze flicked to where his fingers rested over his sternum.

"I can't forget this bionic prosthetic arm," Ray marveled as he raised his prosthesis for Simetra's inspection.

Simetra's gaze held admiration at how realistic the synthetic sleeve fit over the titanium in Ray's arm. He flexed his fingers for good measure.

 "Are you still doing electrical work?"

"I'm a glutton for punishment." A wry smile tugged at his lips. "On a break from my latest job—right here in the hospital. Psychiatric floor. They asked me to repair the boxes and switches that got damaged."

Simetra straightened. "I was curious about the accident, so I went up to the shock therapy suite…" She hesitated, shaking her head. "But I didn't really know what I was looking at. Did you notice anything that seemed off?"

Ray scoffed, folding his arms. "The whole damn thing was suspicious."

Her pulse kicked up. "What do you mean?"

He exhaled, rubbing his jaw. "A few days ago, I was in one of the rooms… Saw a nurse with a patient." His gaze darkened, his expression sharpening. "They were both acting weird."

Ray exhaled slowly, shaking his head. "I heard later the patient was electrocuted."

Simetra stiffened. "Have you talked to anyone else about what you saw?"

He rubbed the back of his neck. "I might've mentioned it to my supervisor."

Before she could ask more, Ray's phone buzzed in his pocket. He glanced at the screen, his brows lifting slightly.

"Speaking of supervisors," he muttered, "that's him right now." He stood, tucking the bill back into his jacket. "I'll be getting back to work."

Simetra nodded, though unease gnawed at her. "If you don't hear from me about the new bill in forty-eight hours, don't hesitate to come back and see me."

Ray flashed a tired but appreciative smile. "I sure appreciate all your help, ma'am."

With that, he stepped out, leaving Simetra alone with far more questions than answers.

CHAPTER 32

Ray Stewart packed up his toolbox, the hum of the electroshock suite settling into quiet. He took a sip from his thermos, the warmth lingering on his lips before he picked up the heavy case and headed for the door.

Then, the pain struck.

A fierce, crushing weight clamped down on his chest. His fingers spasmed, the toolbox slipping from his grip as his knees buckled. He gasped—once, twice—before the world tilted violently, and he crashed forward onto the cold floor.

Ray opened his eyes to fluorescent glare. The sterile scent of antiseptic filled his nose. Machines beeped softly around him, their rhythmic pulses keeping time with the IV drip attached to his arm.

His head was elevated, his body weak but aching with the memory of what had happened. He brought his phone to his ear, his voice hoarse.

"I don't know what happened. My legs gave out. Woke up in the E.R. Doctor says I had a heart attack."

The blood pressure cuff tightened on his arm, squeezing as it measured his racing pulse.

Then, before he could process the thought, his chest seized.

The defibrillator fired.

His breath hitched. **"Oh God."**

The second shock tore through him. His body flew backward, his muscles convulsing in violent protest. His eyes stretched wide—panicked, pleading—before the monitors around him exploded into chaos.

Alarms shrieked. Numbers flashed, and then—darkness.

One by one, the machines shut down.

A nurse rushed in, hitting the call button hard. **"Code Blue! ER Stat! Code Blue ER Stat!"**

Hands worked feverishly, lowering the bed, searching for a pulse that wasn't there. CPR began, chest compressions deep and desperate.

More nurses and doctors flooded the room, wheeling in the crash cart. A syringe plunged into his veins—epinephrine, a last-ditch attempt.

The AED fired. Once. Twice.

No response.

Minutes passed, stretching into eternity.

The doctor lowered his head, the weight of finality settling in his voice.

"Time of death… 3:00 PM."

CHAPTER 33

Simetra placed her laptop, purse, and a to-go box into the back seat of her car, moving with practiced efficiency. The parking lot was quiet — a little too quiet.

A noise.

Her head snapped around, searching the dimly lit space. Nothing.

With a breath, she slid into the driver's seat and backed out of the parking space.

Then—a bump.

Her heart leapt as she slammed the brakes, eyes darting to the rearview mirror.

Cecil.

She threw the door open, rushing toward him. He was doubled over. His arms wrapped around his midsection where the car had caught him. The black bag he'd been clutching lay at his feet.

"Cecil! Are you alright?"

He sucked in a breath, steadying himself. "I've been better."

Simetra's gaze swept over him, scanning for injuries. "Jeezus, boy! I didn't know what to think when I saw it was you."

Cecil straightened, flashing a pained smile. "No harm done, Mama. I was hoping to see you—I brought you something."

He bent down, picking up the bag, but Simetra hesitated.

She thought she heard something—just beyond the cars, near the pillars—but the lot remained still.

She shook off the unease and grabbed Cecil's arm, urgency creeping into her voice.

"Let's get out of here."

Neither of them saw the figure lingering in the shadows—a man in a mask and a black ball cap, watching from behind one of the pillars.

Simetra pulled into the driveway, the familiar shape of her home in Newport News casting long shadows beneath the porch light. As she shifted the car into park, she glanced at Cecil, offering a tired smile.

"You're going to have to pardon the mess," she said, exhaling. "I've let this place go since I started getting Nevell's place ready for him to come home."

Cecil shrugged. "It can't be that bad. Trust me—on the streets, I've seen much worse."

Simetra chuckled, shaking her head. "I got something for you in the trunk. Grab that box while I get your dinner."

She moved to the back of the car, lifting the trunk with practiced ease. The scent of warm food drifted up as she retrieved the to-go box, snapping the lid shut before closing the trunk.

Cecil pulled out a large box, shifting its weight as he stood up straight.

Together, they climbed the steps, the wooden planks creaking beneath their feet. The door swung open, revealing the quiet interior, welcoming, despite the clutter.

Home.

Cecil pulled sweaters and shirts from the box, his fingers brushing against soft fabric. Simetra approached, setting a to-go plate on the table before her gaze landed on the worn black bag on the floor.

"What's that you dropped over there?"

Cecil bent down, grabbed the bag, and pulled open the zipper. His expression turned somber.

"It's a bunch of stuff that belonged to Ole Spence," he murmured. "I can't find him no more, so I brought it to you—hoping you'd seen him and knew where he was."

Simetra frowned, watching as Cecil sifted through the contents.

"Mama, just so you know," Cecil said, voice low, "Ole Spence was digging through garbage and panhandling… but he didn't need to."

He pulled out a battered wallet, flipping it open to reveal an unsettling handful of credit cards. Simetra took the wallet from him, fingers carefully extracting Spencer's ID and a crisp bank deposit receipt.

She scanned the numbers and froze.

"Look at all them zeros, Mama," Cecil whispered, eyes wide. "Ole Spence stacked a bank and never even touched it."

Simetra's grip tightened around the slip of paper.

"Where could he have gotten all this money?"

Simetra's fingers tightened around Spencer's ID, her mind racing. "He was admitted to the hospital as indigent when he had ID and resources all along."

Cecil shifted uneasily. "Don't get mad, Mama." He hesitated, rubbing the back of his neck. "Ole Spence had a watch in there too, but…I sold it. Used the money to get a room and some food for a few days."

Simetra let out a slow breath, staring at him. "You know this is one of those moments where, if I were your real Mama, I'd go upside your head."

Cecil instinctively took a step back, eyes wary. "I know I was wrong, but—"

She sighed, shaking her head. "I'm not agreeing with what you did, but I understand why. Besides… Spencer isn't going to need it anymore."

Cecil frowned, his gaze dropping to the to-go plate she had just set down. "I noticed you didn't bring him one." He looked up, expression searching. "He's not coming back, is he?"

Simetra swallowed, the weight of her words settling deep in her chest. "No, Cecil, he's not."

Cecil's face hardened, his voice quieter now. "Spencer is dead?"

She nodded.

"What happened to him?"

Simetra exhaled, staring at the old wallet in her hands. "It's a long story. He died at the hospital… undergoing treatment for his paranoia."

Silence stretched between them, heavy and unyielding.

Simetra took the bag from Cecil, weighing it in her hands.

"What else is in here?"

She reached inside, fingers brushing against worn fabric and scattered papers. Then, she felt something ratty, a crumpled envelope tucked deep within.

Pulling it free, she slid her thumb beneath the flap and carefully peeled it open.

Inside was a single sheet of paper. The ink was smudged, the edges stained, as if it had been handled too many times. Names and phone numbers filled the page, some barely legible.

But one stood out.

At the very top, **Nevell Carter**.

Simetra froze, her grip tightening, heart hammering against her ribs.

"Mama? You alright?" Cecil's voice pulled her back.

Her throat felt dry as she whispered, "Nevell and Spencer knew each other."

Cecil let out a low chuckle, shaking his head. "You know what they say about it being a small world."

Simetra stared at the paper, her stomach twisting.

"And just like that, it just got even smaller."

CHAPTER 34

Simetra sat at the dining room table, her laptop open, the glow of the screen casting a reflection on her tired eyes. Across from her, Cecil finished the last bite of his pot roast, wiping his mouth before stretching back in his chair.

An email popped onto Simetra's screen—an attachment. She clicked, but a security prompt appeared.

"I hate when people send you emails that go through Google," she muttered, frustrated. "Then you need a password, and by the time I get through all that, I don't even want to read it."

Cecil pushed his plate aside and stood. "Let me take a look, Mama."

Simetra shot him a pointed glance. "Lose the 'Mama.' Makes me sound old."

Smirking, Cecil slid into the chair beside her and took over on the laptop. His fingers flew across the keyboard, navigating past the security screen with ease.

"Voilà!" he said triumphantly. "You needed to use the QR code to bypass the password."

Simetra blinked. "I didn't know you had skills."

Cecil gave a short laugh, his expression dimming slightly. "Before my life went to shit, I studied computers at William and Mary."

Simetra leaned back, considering him. "You ever thought about getting a job? Starting over?"

Her words hung in the air, weighty.

Cecil hesitated, running a hand through his hair. "I think about it all the time."

"Mama, they got me on so many prescription meds I'm a high risk for disaster on a nine-to-five." Cecil's voice was steady, but there was an edge to it—an admission laced with resignation.

Simetra folded her arms. "You could change that. I'll help you."

Cecil walked to the front door, his steps slow, thoughtful. Simetra followed close behind, watching him.

He paused at the threshold, glancing back with a teasing grin. "You sure you don't want to be my mama?" He chuckled before shaking his head. "If you don't get out of here—"

Simetra smirked but said nothing. Cecil stepped off the porch, his silhouette illuminated by the streetlight filtering through the trees.

Simetra flipped the switch for the porch light. Nothing.

She frowned, tapping it again, but the bulb remained dark.

Beside the house, shadows shifted.

Cecil saw it too. Something was moving in the trees. He didn't pause, didn't react beyond a quick glance before continuing through the yard, heading toward the street.

Simetra lingered, eyes scanning the quiet neighborhood, searching for anything out of place.

Then, just beyond the trees, tucked deep in the darkness, a figure stood masked in shadow, watching the house.

Simetra's breath hitched, but before she could focus, the moment slipped away.

She took one final look outside, then closed the door.

Cecil moved like a ghost, feet light on the ground as he closed the distance between himself and the figure standing in the yard.

With one swift motion, he swung the stick hard, connecting with the man's back.

A sharp grunt escaped the stranger's lips before he crumpled forward, his limbs folding beneath him as he hit the ground.

Cecil wasted no time. He grabbed the man beneath his arms and began dragging him toward the porch, straining against the dead weight.

Then—movement.

The bushes beside the house rustled, faint but undeniable.

Cecil froze, eyes narrowing as he scanned the darkness.

Nothing.

Just crickets. Just the hum of the night.

But someone was there.

Unbeknownst to Cecil, the masked man had melted into the shadows, pressing himself tight against the house beneath the living room window.

Cecil cocked his head, listening…waiting. There was nothing but silence.

After a long pause, he exhaled and went back to struggling with the man at his feet, unaware that danger still lurked just beyond the streetlight.

CHAPTER 35

Levi sat on the sofa in the dimly lit living room, pressing an ice pack to the back of his head. Simetra perched beside him, arms folded, a sharp look in her eyes.

"What were you thinking, lurking around out there in the dark?" she demanded.

Levi exhaled, shifting the ice pack. "I thought I saw somebody hanging around the place."

Cecil stood by the door, hands shoved in his pockets, trying—failing—to look innocent.

"Bruh! My bad." He offered a sheepish grin. "I hope you're not gonna arrest me or anything?"

Levi leveled him with a dry stare. "I should. You assaulted a police officer."

Cecil blinked, then scoffed. "How was I supposed to know? You didn't have on a uniform."

Silence hung for a beat before Simetra sighed, shaking her head. "I swear, you two are gonna give me gray hairs."

Simetra crossed her arms, standing firm despite the unease creeping up her spine. Levi gave her a reassuring nod.

"Ms. Thomas," Levi said, his voice steady but urgent. "I came here to update you on Mr. Carter's investigation."

Simetra's expression became hopeful. "Did you find the driver of the truck that hit Nevell?" "Not yet," said Levi. "But we've determined that your brother's accident was no accident. The driver of the truck deliberately tried to kill your brother after hitting him."

Simetra's knees buckled, and she grabbed the back of a nearby chair to keep from falling.

"Do you know anyone who would want to harm your brother?"

Simetra and Cecil shared a look that didn't go unnoticed by Levi Stone.

Simetra wasn't sure if she could trust Levi with her suspicions that Spencer's death and Nevell's accident were related. She had to throw off his suspicions.

"So that person is not just eluding arrest, he's waiting for a second chance to kill my brother," said Simetra. Her voice echoed the desperate realization of the situation.

"I'm sorry, but you're correct. We've placed round-the-clock police around your brother at the hospital. I wanted to make you aware before you came to visit Mr. Carter."

"That's very kind of you, Detective Stone."

"I want you to know that your life could also be in danger. The safest option would be to stay at your brother's place. It has cameras and a state-of-the-art security system."

"I'd rather stay in my home for now," determination underlined Simetra's fear.

"I could sleep a lot easier knowing you were somewhere secure." Levi was just as determined.

Simetra sighed, shaking her head. "I promise I'll get cameras installed here, too, okay? Besides, Nevell's place is too big for me to stay there alone. I don't plan to move in until I bring him home."

Levi studied her, frustration flickering in his sharp gaze. She could tell he wanted to press the issue, but she was firm in her decision. She wasn't about to uproot her life, even if danger lurked in the shadows.

A shadow loomed in the dim glow of the porch light, barely visible beyond the edge of the yard. The man stood still—too still—his masked face angled toward the living room window. Silent. Watching.

The faint outline of his breath fogged against the cool night air as he observed the scene inside. Was he waiting? Calculating? Simetra's pulse quickened, though she wasn't even aware of his presence yet.

Outside, beneath the weight of darkness, the man didn't move.

CHAPTER 36

The Great Escape Day Spa lived up to its name. Simetra reclined in a zero-gravity chair, the gentle hum of soft music wrapping around her like a cocoon. The chilled cucumber water in her hand sent cool relief through her fingertips with every sip.

Beside her, Phyllis sighed into her own chair, sinking into the luxurious stillness. The room was bathed in low, ambient light, perfect for shutting out the outside world.

"This feels wonderful," Simetra murmured, letting the weight of the chair hold her. "But I feel so guilty taking the day off to reconnect."

Phyllis scoffed, rolling her head toward Simetra with a knowing look. "Me? I'd be guilt-free." A pause. Then her voice softened. "Soon enough, you're going to have Nevell at home full time."

Simetra exhaled, shifting slightly. "You're right. One of the first things we discussed in my caregiver support group was making time for myself. But technically, I'm not a caregiver yet."

Phyllis turned slightly, raising a brow. "How do you figure that? You're making all of Nevell's medical decisions, handling his finances—you deserve to escape for a month."

Simetra let out a short laugh, shaking her head. "Today is going to have to suffice."

She closed her eyes, allowing herself just a few more stolen moments of peace.

"I booked us an appointment for the works," Simetra said, a grin tugging at her lips. "Steam, mud, massages… mani-pedis. I want to totally unwind."

Phyllis chuckled, swirling the chilled water in her glass before taking a sip. "Thanks for taking a sister with you. You have to admit—it feels good to experience how the other half lives."

Simetra lifted her glass, meeting Phyllis's with a soft clink. They shared a knowing glance, both settling deeper into their chairs, letting the quiet luxury of the spa wash over them.

Hidden behind the towel rack, Devona adjusted her grip on her phone. The soft glow of the screen illuminated the edges of her robe as she snapped photos, carefully staying unseen.

Simetra exhaled, sinking further into the zero-gravity chair. "I could get used to this now that I get an allowance for Nevell's care." She swirled the cucumber water in her glass, watching the condensation bead along the rim.

Phyllis let out a knowing chuckle. "When you get Nevell situated, you should think about a road trip. Since I've met you, I don't think I've ever heard you talk about traveling anywhere."

Simetra scoffed lightly, shaking her head. "I've always worked."

Phyllis leaned back, crossing one leg over the other, her voice soft but firm. "It's time to live it up, Doll. You never know how long you have."

Simetra's brows knit together as she studied Phyllis, a flicker of uncertainty crossing her face. "Live it up?" she echoed, setting her glass down.

Phyllis smirked, her tone light but laced with meaning. "Yes, Doll. You've been handling Nevell's affairs, carrying all this weight—

don't you think it's time to do something just for you?"

Simetra hesitated, fingers absently tracing the condensation on her glass. The idea felt foreign, almost indulgent. Before she could respond, she glanced toward the towel rack—something felt… off.

Simetra tilted her head, considering the thought. But beyond the warm glow of the spa, unseen eyes lingered—watching.

Devona stopped taking pictures and opened up a video instead.

CHAPTER 37

The afternoon light filtered through the blinds in Damon O'Neal's office, casting faint shadows across his desk. Simetra sat beside him, both focused on the computer screen as the Zoom meeting carried on. The moderator's face filled the screen, his tone steady and formal.

"Fellow shareholders, we've covered a lot of material today. I'd like to thank you for your patience. I'm going to give you a few minutes, then ask you to type your votes in the chat."

A stretch of quiet followed. Simetra reached for her notepad, jotting down a quick message before sliding it over to Damon. He glanced down, reading her words before picking up his own pen. His response was brief but telling. He leaned back slightly, offering the camera a composed smile.

Simetra kept her face neutral, resisting the urge to react. The other shareholders could see them…watching and interpreting. Her fingers hovered over the keyboard for a moment before she finally typed her vote into the chat.

The moderator's voice carried through the speakers with practiced finality.

"Thank you again, everyone, for your votes. The recording of this meeting will be sent to your emails. That's all I have for now— enjoy the rest of your evening."

The Zoom screen flickered as Damon exited the meeting. He leaned back in his chair, folding his arms as he regarded Simetra.

"Thanks for asking my advice on how to vote," he said, a faint smirk playing at the corner of his lips. "With all the shareholders watching."

Simetra exhaled, pushing back slightly from the desk, her fingers drumming against her notepad. "I've never done anything like this before. You guys say, 'vote Nevell's proxy' like it's no big deal, but I'm uncomfortable making decisions like this."

Damon let out a quiet chuckle, shaking his head. "Well, you better start getting comfortable." He gathered a few papers, neatly stacking them before sliding them into a folder. "And while you're at it—work on your poker face. You need to decide how you're going to vote before the meeting tomorrow."

With that, he closed down his computer, grabbing his briefcase and pushing back from his desk. The weight of responsibility settled heavily on Simetra's shoulders as she watched him pack up, realizing just how much was at stake.

Damon's tone was firm, his expression serious. "How you vote on the companies presented in the next meeting is super important," he said, his eyes locking onto Simetra's.

Simetra shifted in her seat, feeling the weight of his words settle over her. "I know," she murmured, her fingers tightening slightly around her pen. "I just want to be sure I'm making the right decision."

Damon exhaled, slipping his laptop into his bag. "Then take the time to really think about it. These votes shape the direction of everything—you don't want to second-guess yourself later."

Simetra nodded slowly, but the unease remained.

CHAPTER 38

Simetra sat at Nevell's desk, her shoulders sagged from the responsibility placed upon them. The notebook lay open before her, its pages filled with details on Midtown Medical Supply. She clicked through the files on Nevell's computer, scanning for anything that stood out.

Then—Apex Biotech.

Her eyes darted between the screen and the notes scribbled in the margins of the notebook. The name appeared in both places, interwoven with Midtown Medical. A manufacturing company. Artificial hearts, ventilators, pacemakers—critical medical devices.

But that wasn't all.

Her pulse quickened as she read further. Apex Biotech had a history, a very troubling one. Lawsuits, devices malfunctioning. The kind of errors that cost lives.

Simetra leaned back, gripping the edge of the desk. This wasn't just business. This was a pattern.

And Nevell had been watching it unfold.

Simetra's eyes darted across the screen, taking in the list of recalled medical devices.

Ventilator—Model T90125: recalled. AED—Model A70184: recalled. Artificial Heart—Model C41288: recalled.

She inhaled sharply, scrolling through the notes. The distribution manager at Apex Biotech had been the one overseeing the recalls.

A sinking feeling settled in her chest as she opened a search tab. Fingers flying over the keyboard, she typed: Distribution Manager, Apex Biotech.

Within seconds, the company's management team appeared. Her pulse quickened as she scanned the names and faces.

CEO. Finance Officer. Production Manager.

Then—her breath hitched.

Distribution Manager.

The photo stared back at her, unmistakable.

Simetra's throat tightened as the name registered. Her fingers curled against the desk.

"Oh my God," she whispered.

Spencer.

Simetra's breath caught in her throat.

The screen illuminated the dim light in Nevell's study, casting a faint glow over the desk as she stared, frozen. **Spencer Walach.** His photo, his name…there, in front of her.

Her pulse pounded as she traced the details in his face, the same sharp blue eyes always seeming to be on the edge of revealing some secret. Here he was the same man who had hovered on the edges of her life, tangled in shadows she hadn't realized were connected.

A chill crept down her spine.

She had found the thing she wasn't supposed to see.

CHAPTER 39

Simetra grabbed her cell phone, fingers trembling slightly as she dialed. The call barely rang once before Damon O'Neal picked up.

"To what do I owe this pleasure?" His voice carried a smooth confidence, the kind that made it impossible to tell whether he was amused or wary.

Simetra didn't waste time. "You knew Nevell was going to dump the stock on the anniversary date because the companies affiliated with Apex Biotech were losing money."

A brief silence stretched between them before Damon responded, his tone measured.

"I see you've been doing your homework."

Simetra tightened her grip on the phone, her pulse pounding. She had discovered something really important. Damon had known all along.

Simetra's grip became even tighter, frustration bubbling beneath the surface. "If you knew, why didn't you just tell me?"

Damon's voice came through the speaker, steady but edged with something unreadable. "As stupid as this may sound, I'm Nevell's lawyer, not yours. I'm risking getting disbarred for even pointing you in the direction to get answers to questions you should ask."

Simetra stared at the screen, her pulse hammering as the weight of his words settled in. He wasn't denying anything. He had known—just like she suspected. And yet, he had kept his distance, held his tongue.

She exhaled sharply, eyes flickering back to the name on the screen. Spencer Walach.

Simetra sighed. This conversation was proving to be pointless. Holding on to the final straw of hope she asked yet another question. "Is there any way you can help me that won't get you into trouble?"

Damon sighed, his voice carrying a familiar edge of restraint. "There is, but it will come at a heavy cost to your brother."

Her pulse quickened. "Did you know that Nevell knew Spencer Walach?"

A pause. Too long.

"There you go again, asking questions I can't answer."

Simetra let out a humorless laugh. "More like won't answer."

A sudden beep interrupted the call from Damon's end.

"I've got another call coming through."

Simetra clenched her jaw. "Thanks for nothing."

She ended the call without waiting for a goodbye, frustration simmering as she stared at her screen.

CHAPTER 40

Dawn unfurls over Lake Maury on the Overlook, casting a fragile glow on the water. Scott Colton stands at the edge of the makeshift pier, staring into the shifting ripples below. The wood beneath his boots groans in protest—some planks are worn thin, gaping at the water beneath. Beside him, a mini cooler sits in silence, untouched.

A presence shifts in the trees. Carla steps forward, her hoodie drawn close, eyes flicking toward him before she lowers herself onto the wooden bench a few feet away. She exhales shakily.

"Mr. Colton… I'm glad you agreed to meet me."

Scott doesn't answer right away. He watches the lake a second longer, as if searching for something beneath the surface, then turns. His footsteps are deliberate as he makes his way back to her, the bench creaking as he sits beside her.

"You sounded shaken on the phone," he says.

Carla grips the hem of her hoodie, knuckles whitening. She scans the trees like something might slip through them. Her voice comes barely above a whisper.

"I'm scared, Mr. Colton. I don't want to die like Justin."

Carla scans the trees before speaking, her voice low, uncertain.

"They say it was an accident, but I don't believe it."

Scott watches her carefully, weighing the fear behind her words. He shifts his stance, rubbing a hand over his face before lowering himself onto the bench beside her.

"I want to help you, but I don't know if I can," he says. His tone is measured, cautious.
"What is it you think I should know? And what, if anything, does it have to do with Spencer Walach's accident?"

Carla hesitates, scanning the overlook as if unseen eyes might linger in the shadows. When she speaks, it's barely above a whisper.

"What happened to Mr. Walach was a nightmare. Justin and I—" her throat tightened, "—we froze. By the time we moved, it was too late to stop him from being shocked."

Scott pulls in a slow breath, listening intently to her words. He stands, crossing the few steps back to the edge of the pier, then kneels to retrieve a bottle of water from the mini cooler. The plastic crinkles in his grip as he twists off the cap, his mind turning over possibilities, the unanswered questions stacking higher.

Scott exhales slowly, rubbing a hand across his jaw. His gaze flicks to Carla, hesitant, watching him like she's measuring his reaction. Finally, he speaks, his voice low but firm.

"You both wound up getting shocked as well. I need you to tell me what happened."

He stands, crossing the few steps back to her, then sits again, pressing a chilled bottle of water into her hands. She takes it, fingers tight around the plastic, but doesn't drink. The cap stays twisted open, untouched.

Carla swallows hard, glancing at the lake before she speaks.

"The electroshock machine didn't do anything the first time I flipped the switch. Nothing at all."

She pulls in a breath, eyes darting as if replaying the scene in her mind.

"The second time—" her voice tightens "—I could hear electricity crackling through my body and felt myself hitting the floor. Before everything went dark, I saw Mr. Walach was moving like a puppet on crack, jerking all over the table. The smell was awful."

Scott watches her, waiting. She's holding something back.

Carla exhales sharply, shoulders tense.

"But what I really need to tell you is what happened later on in the shift."

Carla tearfully relives the scene that day.

The Psych Ward at Mercy Hospital hums with a sterile stillness, the air thick with the lingering weight of grief. Carla Benyon stands in the corner, arms wrapped tightly around herself, silent except for the soft tremor of her breath. Her tears slip down her cheeks, unnoticed, unacknowledged.

Justin Ambrose helps the orderly drape a crisp white sheet over Spencer Walach's lifeless form. The fabric settles gently, concealing what remains. Together, they wheel him toward the exit, the sound of the rolling cart pressing into the hush of the room.

Carla doesn't move. She watches, but she does not follow.

The door swings open again—this time, a housekeeper. She hums under her breath as she pushes her cleaning cart into the space, a practiced motion, almost indifferent to the scene before her. She moves with efficiency, breaking down the electroshock machine, her hands swift and methodical. No hesitation. No lingering pause.

Without a word, she stashes it onto her cart, turns, and wheels it away.

Carla exhales, gripping the bottled water like an anchor. Her voice is tight, controlled—but beneath it, the weight of disbelief lingers.

"I went back to the ward just to prove to myself that the nightmare really happened— that I didn't dream it."

She swallows, then quickly looks toward Scott with her gaze settling on the lake.

"When I got there, the shock machine was back in the suite. It was all burned up… but even more burned than the last time I saw it."

A beat of silence stretches between them. Then, slowly, Carla lifts the bottle to her lips, taking a drink at last.

Scott watches her carefully, brow furrowing as his mind turns over the details. His voice is quiet, measured.

"Why would the housekeeper take the machine out… and then someone bring it back?"

The water bottle slips from Carla's fingers, landing at her feet with a thump. "I don't know," she answered Scott. Unease clawed at her gut. She scanned the dark water lapping beneath the pier. Something was off.

"We need to find that housekeeper," she murmured.

Seconds stretched. Her pulse slowed, then surged—her vision swam. The world tilted at a sickening angle.

"What... was in that water?"

Scott Colton stood still, watching—his expression unreadable.

She staggered toward him, grasping for balance. But he moved first. A sudden shift—side-stepping her reach. In one swift motion, he yanked up a loose plank from the pier.

The wood connected hard.

White-hot pain seared her forehead. The impact sent her sprawling into the freezing water below.

Shock stole her breath. She splashed, gasping, cold, swallowing her limbs. Her fingers scrabbled against the slick wood of the pier, desperate for grip.

But Scott Colton wasn't done.

The plank pressed against her skull. Firm. Unrelenting.

"You've been a bad girl, Carla." His voice was calm. "You should've stayed hidden."

Her body jerked. Thrashing. Water surged over her, forcing its way into her lungs.

Then—a slowing. A fading.

The struggle ceased.

Her body drifted, limp, against the pier.

Scott exhaled, flicking the plank into the water.

CHAPTER 41

Levi Stone stepped into Scott Colton's office without hesitation. The room smelled of polished wood that Levi hadn't noticed before.

Scott sat behind his desk, legs crossed, fingers drumming against the armrest. A lazy smirk tugged at his lips, but his eyes were sharp, even calculating.

"To what do I owe the pleasure?" His voice, thick with sarcasm, curled around the words like smoke.

Levi didn't bother with pleasantries. He stood firm, his presence pressing against the space between them.

"I really had you pegged for being involved in Spencer Walach's death."

Scott sighed, shaking his head as if Levi had just uttered something tedious.

"Oh, for God's sake—can't we let this madness die already? Spencer Walach had an accident." His tone was exasperated, dismissive, but Levi caught the subtle tension in his posture—the slight tightening of his jaw.

"If you'd let me finish," Levi continued, voice steady, "I'm actually here about Carla Benyon."

Silence.

Scott's fingers stopped drumming.

"What about her?" His voice came out too carefully, as though he thought about each word before speaking.

Levi took a slow step forward.

"Her body turned up near the overlook at Lake Maury."

Another beat of silence. The air grew heavier.

Levi tilted his head slightly, watching for the shift—the flicker of unease.

"You know," he murmured, "it's odd. Everyone tied to Spencer Walach's accident… they all wound up dead. From accidents, of course."

He let the words linger. He wanted Scott to feel them, to sit with the implication.

Scott didn't move. But something in his expression shifted—barely perceptible, but enough.

Levi smiled, but it wasn't friendly.

"I've launched a full investigation into all three deaths." His voice held no room for negotiation. "Not cooperating with us? Not an option."

He didn't wait for a reply. He turned, walking out, leaving the weight of his presence behind.

Scott remained still for a long moment. Then, slowly, he exhaled.

His hand moved to the receiver on his desk, fingers curling around it before bringing it to his ear.

"Devona," he said, voice low, sharp. "Get in here. Now."

Devona strutted into Scott Colton's office, her heels clicking against the hardwood with practiced precision. She played the part well—the seductive assistant, the woman used to having men trip over themselves to indulge her.

Scott barely looked up.

She leaned over his desk, deliberately exposing too much cleavage, her voice dripping with suggestion.

He remained unfazed.

"This cop is starting to get on my nerves," Scott muttered, finally breaking the silence. "I need you to find out if he's been talking to Simetra Thomas."

Devona let out an exaggerated sigh, rolling her eyes toward the ceiling.

"Why do you even keep her around?" she grumbled. "She's practically begging to have the hospital take the fall for Spencer Walach's death."

Scott leaned back, watching her carefully, his expression unreadable.

"Got to keep my enemies close," he mused.

Then, without warning, his hand shot out, fingers tightening around Devona's throat.

She gasped, startled, nails instinctively flying to his wrist. But Scott wasn't squeezing hard, not yet. Just enough to make his point clear.

"Make sure she doesn't have anything stashed away in her office that could incriminate me," he murmured, voice dangerously low. "You know what will happen if you let me down."

The threat hung between them, heavy, unspoken.

Scott released his grip, slowly, deliberately.

Devona swallowed, composing herself, smoothing a hand over her blouse like she hadn't just been caught off guard.

She offered a small, tight smile, but Scott wasn't fooled.

Neither of them spoke as she turned and walked out.

CHAPTER 42

The house was quiet, save for the intermittent shrill beep of the heart monitor beside Nevell's bed. Evening shadows stretched across the walls, casting long, creeping lines over his still form.

Simetra sat beside him, fingers wrapped around his hand, her thumb tracing small circles against his skin. His eyes remained closed, his breathing steady but fragile.

"I know you can hear me, Bubba," she whispered, leaning in. "I need you to do something for me."

Her voice wavered, but she held firm. She had to.

"You know what I need you to do? I need you to wake up."

Silence. No response.

Simetra sighed softly, her other hand reaching to caress his cheek, gentle, desperate. She refused to break, refused to let doubt consume her. But the weight of Dr. Rossmore's words sat on her chest like a stone. He had written Nevell off. She hadn't.

She swallowed hard.

"It's no joke keeping up with your investments and everything," she murmured, trying to fill the void with words, with life. "Damon is determined to have me do this on my own. He's quick to say he'll help, but it's always me making the decisions. Like I know what I'm doing."

Her gaze flickered to Nevell's chest, watching the slow, rhythmic rise and fall. No ventilator. That had to mean something. That had to mean hope.

"I wish you could tell me how you got involved with Spencer Walach." Her voice dipped lower now, contemplative. "Detective Stone seems to think his accident wasn't an accident. Maybe neither was yours."

A chill ran through her.

Carefully, she reached for the blanket, pulling it higher over Nevell's chest, a small gesture of comfort.

"I've got to run out for a minute," she whispered, brushing her fingertips over his hand one last time. "Your nurse is right outside. I'll see you in a few."

With one final glance, she stood, exiting the room with a reluctant step.

As the door clicked shut behind her, Nevell's eyelids fluttered. His fingers twitched against the blanket.

The door eased open, and Nevell's nurse stepped inside, her movements deliberate, controlled. The soft hum of medical equipment filled the room, punctuated by the occasional beep of the heart monitor.

She approached the bed, her crisp white uniform and her hair pulled back in a severe bun made her look like a robot. Her back was ramrod straight as she adjusted his trach with exaggerated care. The touch should have been gentle, reassuring. Instead, it felt clinical. Cold.

Nevell's fingers twitched.

She froze.

Slowly, her gaze flickered to his hand, watching the slight movement—too slight to mean anything, or maybe too significant to ignore.

Her expression remained unreadable.

Without hesitation, she pivoted, crossing the room in a few crisp steps. At the window, she pulled out her phone, pressing it to her ear.

"It's me," she murmured, her voice low, firm.

She turned back to Nevell, eyes sharp, gaze assessing. The look wasn't one of concern; it was one of calculation.

"He might be coming around," she said, voice steady, final.

She gave no clue to whoever was on the other end of the call. Her words settled like lead in the room.

Nevell remained motionless, but his fingers twitched again.

CHAPTER 43

Down the hall, Nevell's study was silent as Simetra navigated the contents of his computer. The glow from the screen cast long shadows across the desk, illuminating only what lay directly in front of her. The rest of the room was shrouded in darkness.

She exhaled slowly, willing her hands to stay steady. This felt intrusive, forbidden, but she had no choice. Nevell wasn't awake to answer her questions, and waiting wasn't an option.

Her fingers flew over the keyboard as she typed: **Spencer Walach**.

A list of emails popped onto the screen.

Her pulse quickened. She clicked the top one.

An attachment.

She opened it.

The image loaded, pixel by pixel—workers stationed along an assembly line, methodically assembling medical supplies. Nothing overtly alarming, but something about it made her uneasy. She closed the attachment, then the email, and moved to the next one.

A message regarding **MidTown Medical Supply's** operations.

Her stomach tightened.

Another attachment. She clicked.

A spreadsheet appeared. Heavy losses for the quarter sprang out at her. The numbers were stark, glaring, painting a picture of financial strain.

Simetra swallowed.

She opened yet another email.

Spencer Walach's name stood out immediately.

"We need to meet face to face," his message read. *"It's about Apex Biotech."*

Apex Biotech.

Simetra sat back, gripping the phone in her lap.

For a moment, she hesitated, staring at the words on the screen, feeling the weight of them settle deep into her bones.

Then, without another thought, she dialed.

The line rang once.

Then again.

She lifted the phone to her ear.

"We have a problem," she said.

Simetra's phone buzzed in her palm the moment she pressed dial. Cecil answered on the first ring.

"What's up, Mama?" His voice came through steady, familiar.

She wasted no time.

"Where are you right now?"

"Not far from your old house," he said, a hint of curiosity in his tone. "What's going on?"

Simetra hesitated for half a second, then pushed forward.

"Meet me there. I'm working on something, and I might need a little backup in case I run into a snag."

Cecil didn't ask questions, didn't probe for details. He never did.

"I'm on my way now," he said simply.

Simetra exhaled, glancing toward the front door.

"I leave the extra key under the yellow flowerpot on the porch in case I lock myself out," she told him. "You can take a shower if you need to. Some of Nevell's old clothes are in the spare bedroom at the top of the stairs."

"Got it," Cecil replied, then hung up.

Simetra stared at her phone for a moment longer. Unsure of what she would find out about Nevell and Spencer, she hurriedly powered down the computer.

CHAPTER 44

Simetra sat at the dining room table in Thomas' home. The glow of the laptop screen cast soft light across the coffee table, illuminating her focused expression. She tapped at the keyboard, pulling up Apex Biotech's homepage, scanning the familiar logo as it loaded.

Footsteps echoed from upstairs.

Cecil emerged, his beard freshly edged, his sides neatly trimmed. His hair was braided into a tight top knot, giving him a sharp, refined look. He wore Nevell's clothes, and somehow, they fit him like they were tailored for him.

Simetra leaned back, taking him in with an approving nod.

"Now that's what I'm talking about."

Cecil grinned, turning slightly to show off his profile, amused by her reaction.

"Glad you like," he said.

Simetra exhaled, her fingers resting against the laptop's edge.

"I'm glad you and Nevell are the same size," she mused, her voice carrying a thread of something unspoken. Then, after a pause, she met his gaze. "I asked you here because I need help searching some files."

Her tone had shifted—less casual, more serious.

Cecil's expression sobered as he stepped closer.

"Alright," he said, lowering himself onto the couch beside her. "What are we looking for?"

Simetra tapped at the keyboard, her eyes fixed on the Apex Biotech homepage. The company's sleek branding filled the screen, pristine, polished, and carefully curated. But she knew better—what was on the surface rarely told the whole story.

Cecil glanced over her shoulder at the screen.

"What kind of files, Mama?"

"Files that belong to Apex Biotech," she said simply, still scrolling.

Cecil studied the page, taking in the corporate jargon, the company divisions listed beneath their umbrella.

"This one is the big fish," Simetra murmured, tapping the screen. "MidTown Medical and MedSouth Medical Supply are both under their control. I need more information than what's on the website."

Cecil leaned back, considering.

"So you want me to hack into their system?"

A slow grin tugged at Simetra's lips.

"Sorta, kinda."

Cecil huffed a quiet laugh, rubbing a hand over his beard.

"What I'll need is a computer that can't be traced to me," he said, glancing at her, "or you, for that matter."

Simetra raised a brow.

"What are you, some kind of computer genius on the run from the government?"

Cecil gave her that look that said she wasn't too far off.

"Sorta, kinda."

Simetra exhaled, shaking her head, a smirk creeping onto her face.

"Well, I'll be damned."

CHAPTER 45

Sunlight streamed through the study's windows, spilling across Nevell's desk where Simetra set down a tray with two cups of coffee, cream, and sugar, just the way Cecil liked it.

He was already at the computer, cracking his knuckles before his fingers flew across the keyboard. His movements were swift, confident, controlled chaos behind the screen.

Simetra pulled open a drawer, retrieving a thumb drive.

"We can save anything important on here," she said, holding it up.

Cecil nodded, his focus unwavering.

"Here goes. We've only got a small window before they start tracking me."

Simetra hovered beside him, watching as lines of code blurred across the screen. Then—a breakthrough.

Firewalls bypassed.

Apex Biotech's files opened before them.

Cecil scrolled, filtering through documents, then quickly began downloading several files—profit-and-loss reports from the combined companies under Apex's umbrella.

"This guy, Trevor Knox…" Cecil murmured, eyes narrowing. "Mama, he is a beast. He's got a group of investors, and you wouldn't believe the money pouring into these companies."

Simetra stiffened.

"What about Nevell?" she asked.

Cecil hesitated for a fraction of a second before exhaling.

"Major player."

Simetra's breath hitched, her fingers tightening around the edge of the desk.

She stared at the screen, at the files spilling across it. In front of her was undeniable proof of Nevell's involvement.

"My God, Nevell… what have you gotten yourself into?"

Simetra was slowly starting to wonder if she knew Nevell at all.

Cecil's fingers flew across the keyboard, navigating deeper into Apex Biotech's hidden files. Lawsuits…so many lawsuits. He skimmed through case after case of faulty equipment, patients harmed or killed.

He clicked through images, each more damning than the last, with faces frozen in pain, medical devices that had failed them when they needed them most.

Then—an alert.

A bright red warning flashed on the screen.

His stomach dropped.

"I gotta shut this party down," he muttered, already working to cover his tracks. "They're on to me."

Simetra stiffened beside him, eyes darting to the screen.

"You've got to get rid of this computer. ASAP."

No hesitation.

She reached down, yanking the hard drive's cord from the wall. The monitor flickered once, then went black.

Still, it wasn't enough.

"What are you waiting for?" Simetra snapped. "Help me dismantle it. You can take it somewhere and burn it."

Cecil didn't argue.

He grabbed the tower, already thinking ahead.

There wasn't a second to waste.

CHAPTER 46

The Mariner's Museum glowed under the soft shimmer of chandeliers, the hum of conversation weaving through the grand space. Simetra and Phyllis moved through the crowd, champagne flutes in hand, the scent of polished wood and aged canvases lingering in the air.

At the entrance, an easel sign read: **LOCAL ARTIST DISPLAY.**

A corner near the doorway showcased bold paintings and intricate sculptures, each piece a statement—raw creativity etched into canvas and stone.

Simetra exhaled, letting herself take in the moment.

"You were right," she murmured, glancing at Phyllis. "This isn't so bad. It's actually kind of nice."

Phyllis smirked, sipping her drink.

"See? Told you."

Simetra let her gaze drift over the artwork, lingering on a painting that pulled at something in her chest.

"I was thinking about supporting a local artist and buying a piece," *she said.* "But they're kind of pricey."

Phyllis rolled her eyes dramatically.

"You're killing me, acting like you don't have money."

"Well, I don't."

Phyllis scoffed.

"Yes, you do. It's about time you started acting like it. It's called newfound wealth. You own Nevell, so embrace it."

Simetra stiffened, her fingers tightening around the delicate stem of her flute.

Own Nevell.

That phrase didn't sit right.

Her eyes flickered across the room, searching for something, anything, to ground herself.

That's when she noticed the woman standing near a large sculpture.

Something about her presence made Simetra pause.

Recognition pulled at Simetra's mind.

The woman—there was something about her posture, the way she held herself just outside the glow of the overhead lights. Familiar.

But before she could place it, the woman moved.

A quick retreat into the shadows.

Simetra's breath hitched, and she instinctively leaned toward Phyllis.

"Please keep your voice down," she murmured, barely above a whisper. "Before you bring attention to us."

Phyllis raised an eyebrow but didn't argue, taking a slow sip of her champagne as they turned away, blending back into the hum of conversation.

Behind them, Devona stepped out from the darkness, her presence sharp and deliberate.

She lifted her phone.

The camera lens caught the light for a fraction of a second, then the faint click of a snapshot.

One picture.

Then another.

Her lips curled into a smirk as she lowered the phone, eyes trailing after Simetra and Phyllis before vanishing into the crowd.

Later on that night, the Newport News Police Department was quiet except for the sounds of desk fans and the occasional shuffle of paperwork. Fluorescent lights buzzed overhead, casting a dull glow across the tiled floor.

A woman entered, her stride confident, deliberate.

Form-fitting dress. High heels that clicked against the tile with every step. Big hair, oversized sunglasses disguise, but not enough to mask her entirely.

Devona.

She approached the cop at the front desk, the same one who had subdued Spencer in the alley.

"Ma'am, how can I help you?"

Without a word, she slid an envelope through the glass partition, making sure her fingers brushed his—just enough to linger, just enough to make the moment stretch.

"Can you please make sure that Detective Levi Stone gets this?" Her voice was smooth, practiced, her expression unreadable behind the dark lenses.

The cop glanced at the envelope, then back at her.

"Ma'am, I'll need you to leave your name and contact information."

Devona barely reacted.

"It's not important."

She turned sharply, her heels clicking rhythmically against the tile as she strode toward the exit, never looking back.

The cop watched her go, then looked down at the envelope resting against the desk.

He could sense that whatever was inside wasn't routine.

CHAPTER 47

The early morning light illuminated Nevell's garage from the door that stood open. Simetra scanned the quiet street from inside the garage. She caught sight of a dark sedan parked just outside Nevell's home. She thought it odd but didn't let her mind dwell on that fact.

Simetra's heels echoed against the polished concrete floor as she stepped deeper into Nevell's private sanctuary of luxury vehicles. The scent of fine leather and motor oil clung to the air, mingling with the crisp morning chill filtering in through the half-open garage door.

She ran her fingertips along the smooth curves of a Rolls-Royce, admiring its deep obsidian finish, before moving past the sleek Jaguar, the bold Bentley, and the roaring promise of the Porsche. The BMW and Lexus sat like silent sentinels, each an emblem of Nevell's refined taste.

One car stood out. The Porsche.

With a sly smirk, she reached for the key hanging on the wall peg. "I know any one of these is too extravagant for work," she murmured to herself, turning the key over in her palm. "But what harm can it do?"

As Simetra slid into the driver's seat, the engine roared to life, a smooth, powerful purr that vibrated through her bones.

Just outside was a shadowy presence. Waiting. Watching.

Her pulse quickened. Without hesitation, she gripped the wheel and pressed her foot to the gas. The Porsche shot forward, tires screeching, as she sped past the sedan and onto the open road, leaving the house in her dust.

The man sat motionless in the driver's seat, his ball cap pulled low over his masked face. The tinted windows shielded him from curious eyes as he lifted the tablet from the passenger seat.

A few taps. A line of coded commands.

The screen flashed green. He easily bypassed the security setup.

The garage door groaned as it began to rise, slow and deliberate, like a beast awakening. Simetra was gone, but he had no interest in her departure. His focus was on what lay beyond the open threshold.

The masked man stealthily navigates through Nevell's home until he reaches his security room. The faint hum of servers filled the air as he stepped inside. The walls were lined with screens displaying a watchful grid of surveillance footage, every angle of the property captured in crisp detail. Large computer towers loomed like sentinels, their steady lights blinking in rhythm with the system's pulse.

He hears a noise outside the door. The doorknob twists from the outside, and the door starts pushing forward.

Whoever had been standing outside was coming into the room.

The masked man didn't waste time. He tapped a sequence of codes on the tablet.

One by one, the screens flickered, then blacked out, their power swallowed into oblivion. The room was plunged into digital darkness. A moment later, alarms shrieked through the house, their piercing wails cutting through the silence like jagged blades.

The door closes, and retreating footsteps can be heard outside.

The sudden noise shattered the tranquility of Nevell's bedroom.

Nevell stirred, his body twitching in rhythm with the blinking glow of his bedside clock. His eyes remained shut.

Nevell's nurse burst into the room, her breath uneven, her pulse hammering in her ears. Nevell convulsed, his body jerking violently against the sheets, his hands clenched, his muscles taut with some unseen force.

A seizure.

Her training kicked in—check for a fever, clear the airway. She scanned the room, frantic, searching for something he could bite down on. Bad idea. That method of treating a seizure had long been outdated.

Simetra took a breath to gather her thoughts, but she was running out of time. Nevell was running out of time.

She opened the control panel above Nevell's head and spoke into the microphone.

"Fire department, emergency assistance,"
she commanded sharply, her voice
activating the hospital bed's rescue system.

The house alarm blared in the distance, its
relentless cry melding with Nevell's strained
movements. And then—silence.

His body stilled.

Too still.

She pressed her fingers to his neck. Nothing.

A cold dread crawled up her spine.

Throwing her weight onto his chest, she
initiated CPR, counting each compression
with trained precision.

Her breath came in quick, sharp gasps as she
fought for him, fought against the invisible
force that had stolen his pulse.

She glanced around, a flicker of
something—unease, calculation—crossing
her features.

And then, the firemen poured into the room,
their boots thudding against the floor as they
rushed to assist.

Behind her steady hands and desperate
efforts, there was something else.

Something she wasn't saying.

Something she didn't want them to see.

CHAPTER 48

Simetra burst into the room, her presence a force of nature—unrelenting, fierce. Her gaze locked onto the nurse, sharp and unforgiving, a silent accusation burning in her eyes.

She didn't waste words. She would have her say later. She turned to the firemen, who stood near Nevell's bed. One of them, a broad-shouldered veteran, met her stare with calm assurance.

"He's out of danger," he said, his voice steady, reassuring. The other fireman, who was younger and full of muscles, exchanged a glance with his partner before catching the nurse's eye. Unspoken words hung between them, something between wariness and understanding.

Simetra barely acknowledged the exchange. Her focus narrowed to Nevell as she moved to his side, pressing her fingers against his hand, feeling the warmth of his skin, the proof that he was still here. A small exhale escaped her lips—relief, although fleeting, was undeniable.

The firemen took their leave, footsteps retreating down the hallway.

And then, Simetra turned.

The nurse stiffened, as if anticipating the storm before it arrived.

"You," Simetra's voice was low, simmering with fury. "You were supposed to—"

Words failed her for a moment, choked back by the pain of everything that had almost been lost.

The nurse swallowed hard. "I—"

Simetra cut her off with a sharp glare, stepping forward, the intensity in her expression leaving no room for retreat.

"You don't get to explain," she seethed. "There's nothing you can say to me right now to justify you not doing your damn job."

The walls of the room seemed to tighten around them. The momentary silence was suffocating.

Nevell's nurse straightened her shoulders, defiance surfacing through her fear.

"I—I was—" she stammered, but Simetra wasn't here for excuses.

"Where were you?" Simetra's voice cut through the space like a blade, sharp and unforgiving. "The alarms went off! You should've been here. How could you just leave him like that?" Her voice caught, strangled by the emotion clawing its way up her throat.

The nurse shook her head, her mouth set in a tight line. "I wasn't—It wasn't my fault. I didn't—"

Simetra advanced, the heat of her anger pressing against the cool air of the room. "You didn't what?" she demanded, eyes narrowing. "Hear them? Care? Decide to show up late and pray no one noticed?"

The nurse took a step back, her grip tightening around the clipboard. "I didn't ignore them," she muttered, but her voice lacked conviction. "I was in another room."

Simetra let out a sharp, humorless laugh. "Another room," she echoed, shaking her head. "That's not good enough."

The beeping monitors filled the silence between them, sterile and indifferent. But the weight of the moment and the unspoken consequences of what had transpired hung thick in the air.

Simetra pulled out her phone, fingers moving swiftly as she dialed the nursing agency. The anger in her voice was sharp… clearly demanding immediate action.

"I need another nurse here. Now," she said, cutting through the pleasantries before they could even begin a reply. "I don't care who, just send someone competent."

The nurse flinched, her face pale, her hands gripping the edge of the counter as if bracing for impact.

Simetra barely spared her a glance as she ended the call. She turned, eyes locked onto the woman who had failed the most basic responsibility—to be there when Nevell needed her.

"Pack your shit and get out," she said, her voice cold and final.

The nurse opened her mouth—perhaps to protest, to beg—but one look at Simetra's expression had her thinking better of it. She fumbled for her bag, moving in stiff, hurried motions, the weight of her dismissal settling like lead in the space between them.

Simetra didn't watch her leave.

She turned back to Nevell, brushing her thumb over his hand, her rage shifting into something quieter. The fire was over. The danger had passed.

There could not be a next time.

CHAPTER 49

The rhythmic crash of waves against the shore was nearly drowned out by the murmur of voices and the occasional crackle of police radios. Officers dotted the grounds of Nevell's sprawling mansion, their dark uniforms a stark contrast against the elegant estate.

Some patrolled the perimeter, their eyes scanning for any signs of disturbance, while others lingered inside, speaking in hushed tones as they secured the space.

Levi Stone arrived with long, determined strides, his sharp gaze sweeping over the scene before finding Simetra standing by the pier. The wind tousled her hair, but she barely seemed to notice, her arms folded tightly across her chest, as though bracing herself against more unseen threats.

"I came as soon as I heard," Levi said, his voice carrying concern as he stepped alongside her.

Simetra let out a breath, her shoulders sagging slightly. "It was terrifying. The alarms blaring, Nevell seizing. It all happened so fast. I wasn't ready for it." Her voice wavered, and Levi could see the exhaustion etched in her expression.

"I had to see for myself that he was okay." Levi's tone was firm, as if the mere act of being present could reassure both Simetra and himself.

She nodded, staring out at the endless stretch of water before them. "I can't be with him every second. That's not possible," she admitted, shaking her head. "And I've decided not to keep the same nurse. We'll still have round-the-clock care, but I want different nurses rotating each shift. No more complacency. No more mistakes."

Levi studied her for a moment before giving a small nod of approval. He understood the pressure of her decision. It had to be overwhelming ensuring Nevell's well-being while navigating her own fears. He reached out, a steadying hand brushing her arm. "You're making the right call, Ms. Thomas."

She allowed herself a fleeting smile, but worry still lingered in her gaze. The pier creaked beneath them as the tide shifted, but neither moved.

Levi's brow furrowed as he let out a slow breath, his gaze fixed on Simetra. The dark water beneath the pier rippled in the moonlight.

"I thought you would've called me yourself," he said, his tone edged with disappointment. "Not have me hearing it through precinct channels." He shook his head, folding his arms across his chest. "I'm a little hurt, Ms. Thomas."

She glanced at him, guilt flickering across her face. "It all happened so fast," she admitted, her voice barely above a whisper. "I wasn't thinking about anything except—" She hesitated, shuddering at the memory of Nevell seizing, the alarms blaring, the sheer panic that had gripped her.

Levi softened, nodding. "I get it. But listen, nothing is going to happen to you or Nevell on my watch. You've got round-the-clock surveillance now. You're both protected."

Simetra exhaled a shaky breath, some of the tension in her shoulders easing. But then Levi shifted the conversation, his expression darkening.

"Carla and Justin are dead. Both key witnesses. We just found Carla's body." His words weighed heavily in the night air.

Simetra inhaled sharply, her pulse quickening. "Carla's body?" she repeated, almost as if saying it aloud might make it less real. "How? When?"

"Just today," Levi confirmed. "It's bad, Ms. Thomas. Someone's cleaning up loose ends."

She pressed her lips together, staring out at the waves rolling in, constant, indifferent, as if the world hadn't just shifted beneath her feet. "I promise I'll be careful," she murmured, though even she wasn't sure what that meant anymore.

Levi studied her for a long moment before nodding. "Good. Because whoever's behind this is not done."

The wind picked up, rattling the pier's wooden planks beneath them. Simetra crossed her arms, bracing herself against the chill, against the uncertainty, against the weight of everything that had unraveled before her.

Simetra's voice was barely above a whisper. "Nevell and Spencer knew each other."

Levi froze. The pier beneath them suddenly felt unsteady, as if the weight of her words had shifted the very ground. He turned to face her fully, his jaw tightening.

"Ms. Thomas," he began, his voice low and sharp, "not only did you fail to call me about the security breach at your brother's home, but now you're telling me—just this minute—that you've been sitting on key information that could help in a murder investigation? What the hell, lady?"

Simetra flinched but held her ground. "It's not like I was hiding it. I just—" she exhaled, frustration and regret battling in her expression. "It didn't feel relevant until— until now."

Levi ran a hand down his face, shaking his head as if trying to physically clear his thoughts. "I'm still trying to get my head around this." His tone had lost its bite, but the exhaustion was palpable. "Nevell and Spencer knew each other. That changes everything."

Simetra nodded, guilt settling deep in her chest.

"I'm going to need to see everything you've got." Levi's voice was firm now, resolute, the detective in him taking over. "Every detail, every interaction. Be honest with me and share whatever you have."

She swallowed hard, hugging herself as the breeze swept through the pier. "Most of the information I have is here in the house."

Levi exhaled, the tension between them shifting into something colder. "Good. Because we're running out of time."

CHAPTER 50

Levi sat at his desk, the glow of the computer screen casting sharp shadows across his face. His fingers tapped absently against the keyboard as he scrolled through the files Simetra had given him, rereading the same fragmented details, the same half-answers. It was sketchy at best—just enough to suggest there was more, but not enough to tell him what.

His gut twisted with unease. She was hiding something. Something big.

He leaned back, exhaling slowly, rubbing a hand across his jaw. Trust between them had always been a delicate balance, but now? Now, it felt like a thread stretched too thin, ready to snap. And if it did—if she kept holding back—he might not be the only one paying the price.

She had to know that. She had to understand what was at stake.

He observed the surveillance monitors in the corner of the room, showing a live feed of Nevell's estate. Officers patrolled the grounds, a protective presence, but protection only went so far when shadows moved in places they couldn't see.

Levi clenched his jaw.

If he and Simetra didn't get past the secrets, the hesitation, the lack of trust—they wouldn't just be chasing ghosts.

They could be one.

Levi leaned back in his chair, exhaling sharply as he stared at the screen in front of him. No matter how many times he tried to piece it together, the connection between Nevell and Spencer Walach remained frustratingly out of reach. He'd started with the basics—what they had in common, where they might have crossed paths. Every lead fizzled out at the same dead end.

The one undeniable link between them was Simetra.

His gut twisted at the thought. Had she known more than she was letting on? Had she unintentionally—or deliberately—kept something from him?

Levi rubbed his temple, shaking off the doubt. He needed more than speculation.

He turned his attention to the grainy security footage playing on his screen. Nevell sat at a corner table in Chihuahua's Restaurant, deep in conversation with Devona Drummond. The way he leaned in, the intensity of his expression, whatever they were discussing, hadn't been casual.

This may be the way in. Maybe Devona had insights Simetra didn't want to share.

Levi pushed away from his desk, reaching for his jacket. He was done chasing ghosts. It was time to talk to someone who actually knew Nevell. Someone who might finally give him the missing piece to this puzzle.

Levi barely let the first ring finish before Shepherd picked up.

"I need you to locate Devona Drummond." His voice was sharp, direct.

A pause. Then Shepherd's voice came through, cautious. "As in right this minute, sir?"

Levi smirked, shifting in his seat. "You're catching on, Shepherd. Keep this up, and I might let you go back out and play with the other officers."

His chuckle lingered in the air, but Shepherd stayed silent.

Levi could hear the tension on the other end. He didn't need Shepherd to be comfortable. He just needed results.

The low hum of traffic filled the car as Levi leaned back against the headrest, waiting.

CHAPTER 51

It had been a week since the security breach at Nevell's mansion. The unease had settled. Simetra was satisfied with the home health nurses tending to Nevell and had finally decided it was time to return to work.

The morning was crisp, the air thick with the scent of damp earth as she stepped onto the driveway. She barely spared a glance at the quiet street, not noticing the dark sedan parked near the edge of the property.

Simetra pulled out of the driveway, her thoughts already on the tasks waiting for her at the office. The sedan remained still.

Then there was movement.

A masked man in a ball cap, shrouded in the stillness of his surroundings, lifted a tablet from the passenger seat. His fingers danced across the screen, bypassing firewalls with ease. A soft beep.

Access granted.

He slid out of the car, moving with purpose, his steps barely audible against the pavement. The breach from a week ago had been a test. This was the real thing.

With calculated precision, he reached the mansion's side door. A small flick of his fingers against the screen, and the lock clicked open.

The house swallowed him whole, its silence welcoming.

The door to Nevell's bedroom creaks open. The soft hinge groan was barely noticeable against the quiet hum of medical equipment.

The tall man in the ball cap and mask moves deliberately, his steps measured, his posture unwavering.

Inside, the nurse leans over Nevell's bedside, adjusting the tube feeding with practiced care, her attention solely on her task.

Unaware of what is about to happen until the masked man's hands tighten around her slim throat from behind. He applies enough pressure to snap her neck. With no effort at all, he tosses her limp body to the floor, then steps over her on his way to Nevell's bedside.

Nevell's breath was shallow, the soft hum of machinery pressing against the edges of his awareness. His eyelids fluttered, then popped open. He struggled against the fog clouding his vision. The world around him was muted. The room filled with blurred shapes blending into the dim light of his bedroom.

A figure loomed above him. Close. Too close.

His sight sharpened just enough to register the details. Fear gripped him at the sight of the ball cap, the masked face, the deliberate stillness in the stranger's posture.

Then, slowly, the man reached up.

Fingers curled around the edge of his mask. He pulled it down in one smooth motion.

MAN IN BALL CAP
"There you are."

His voice was edged with something dangerous.

"I'm sure I'm the last person you wanted to see."

Nevell's pulse skipped, his body still too weak to react. But his mind had no choice but to comply.

The mask had been a barrier, a false anonymity. Now, exposed, the man's face unlocked something buried deep within Nevell's mind.

Recognition struck like a sudden bolt of lightning.

He had seen that face before.

CHAPTER 52

Nevell's mind drifts off in a memory of a moment in Deer Park.

The soft ripple of Lake Maury stretched into the horizon, the water catching flecks of sunlight between the swaying branches overhead. Nevell paced at the water's edge, his movements tight with barely contained frustration.

Across the way, Spencer Walach emerged from the direction of the bird habitat, walking with measured steps. He was clean-cut, polished. His polo shirt crisp, khakis unwrinkled, as if he were walking into an office meeting instead of into a secret rendezvous on a park trail.

Nevell kept his distance, his body angled just enough to signal wariness.

"I appreciate the risk you're taking by meeting with me," Nevell said, his voice low.

Spencer exhaled, his gaze shifting briefly to the water before settling back on Nevell.

"It was my duty to warn you about what takes place at the warehouse at Midtown Medical," he replied. "It even happens at Vista Medix and MedSouth."

Nevell's breath hitched—an almost imperceptible pause before he squared his shoulders.

"It couldn't be just one," he murmured, as if saying it aloud would make it less real. "It had to be all three of the companies I have money invested in."

The realization sank deep, heavy like a stone cast into the lake before them.

Nevell's jaw tightened as he stared at Spencer. The revelation felt like a boulder on his chest.

"What are you going to do now that you know the companies are selling devices that have been rebuilt from recalled or damaged products?" Spencer asked, his voice calm but edged with urgency.

Nevell exhaled slowly, eyes narrowing. "There's not much I can do just on your word." He shook his head. "What happened to the devices you promised to bring with you?"

Spencer shifted his stance, glancing briefly toward the distant tree line as if measuring his next words carefully.

"Going into the warehouse with the administrative staff still in the building was too risky." His voice was steady, but there was an underlying frustration. "I'll get you the evidence you need, but it'll have to be after hours—when the workers get sloppy."

Nevell's brow furrowed. The plan was reckless, dangerous.

"That sounds too dangerous." His voice lowered, searching for another angle. "Maybe we can find another way."

The tension between them lingered, the quiet ripple of the lake barely breaking the weight of the conversation.

Spencer looks around nervously, his eyes holding an urgency that couldn't be ignored.

"Unsuspecting patients and their families are putting their lives in danger." His voice was firm, conviction woven into every syllable. "I owe it to them to stop this from going any further."

Nevell studied him, arms crossed, the weight of the situation settling between them.

"You know that when the lid blows off, you won't have a job," Nevell said, his voice quieter now, edged with something close to warning.

Spencer smirked—small, knowing. "Don't worry about me, Mr. Carter." He shifted his weight slightly. "I've got a few pennies squirreled away. I won't go hungry."

Nevell sighed, rubbing a hand over his jaw. He wasn't sure whether Spencer understood just how deep this all ran—but then again, maybe he did. Maybe that was why he was willing to risk everything.

"Contact me when you have the evidence I can give to the other shareholders." His gaze was steady, purposeful. "But above all, be careful."

Spencer gave a small nod, his expression unreadable.

A few feet away, just beyond Nevell's line of sight, a man in a ball cap and dark outfit stood by the water's edge, tossing bits of bread to the turtles.

His movements were unhurried, deliberate.

Watching.

CHAPTER 53

A massive Rottweiler sat at attention beside the man, its sleek black coat gleaming under the fading sunlight. Its posture was rigid and disciplined. Clearly, the dog was trained for something far beyond companionship.

Nevell adjusted his pace as he walked past, casting a fleeting glance at the dog before shifting his focus back to the water's edge.

The man in the ball cap never turned, never acknowledged him. He remained fixated on tossing breadcrumbs into the lake, his movements methodical, precise.

Nevell hesitated, then took a small step toward the animal.

The man in the ball cap didn't look up, didn't stop tossing bread to the turtles.

"What a beautiful dog," he murmured, his voice measured, nonthreatening.

The Rottweiler's ears twitched, but it didn't soften. Instead, a deep, rumbling growl vibrated from its chest, low and deliberate—a warning.

Nevell instinctively took a step back, every fiber in his body urging caution.

The man continued his silent ritual, tossing another piece of bread.

Nevell forced his expression neutral, quickly pivoting, his strides increasing in speed as he moved in the opposite direction.

Behind him, he heard the faintest shift of fabric. The man's hand lowered to rest atop the Rottweiler's head.

The dog's ears twitched again. Her muscles coiled beneath the man's touch.

"Good girl, Callie." His voice was soft, almost affectionate. Then, with slow precision, he stroked the Rottweiler's head.

But beneath it, there was something else.

Something calculated.

Something meant to be heard.

The masked man's movement in the room brings Nevell back to the present.

Nevell tries to scream for help, but no sounds come out. His body also doesn't respond when he tries to move. The fearful recognition in Nevell's eyes excites the man.

But his voice—low, steady, dangerously calm—cut through the quiet like a blade.

"You were too smart for your own good."

The words lingered, hanging in the air between them.

"Too bad you have to learn the hard way that when you mess with a mutha fucker's money, you get his attention."

He finally turned his head—just slightly, just enough.

"You don't want to get my attention."

The quiet stretched, thick with unspoken consequences.

The man in the ball cap slides Nevell's pillow from behind his head and covers his face with it.

Nevell's hands grip the man's wrists. He struggled in vain as the man squeezed the air from his lungs. Slowly, Nevell's grip loosens. His hands drop limply on the bed. His feet no longer kicked the air. The room was deathly quiet as Nevell took his final breath.

CHAPTER 54

Simetra's shoulders sagged with exhaustion as she eased her car into the dimly lit gas station. The neon glow of the flickering sign buzzed overhead, cutting through the stillness of the late evening. The day seemed endless. A hot bath was calling her name.

She just needed gas. Luckily, home was just a few miles away.

She stepped out of the Benzo and made her way inside the gas station to pay. The station was eerily quiet. No cashier stood at the register. No customers lingered in the aisles. Something about the emptiness sent a ripple of unease through her, but before she could call out, she caught sight of the small television mounted behind the counter.

Her breath hitched.

On the screen, her own face stared back at her. Her own image was unsettling. Next to it on a split screen, Nevell's face. A deep voice filled the silence, crackling through the speakers like a ghost in the quiet store.

"Local businessman Nevell Carter was found murdered earlier this afternoon. Police

have identified their prime suspect…
Simetra Thomas."

The words slammed into her, knocking the air from her lungs. The station seemed to tilt, the fluorescent lights suddenly too bright. Her pulse pounded in her ears, drowning out everything.

She still didn't see anyone, which made what she was hearing sound even more like something out of *The Twilight Zone*. Simetra gasped. "No! No! No!" she yelled as panic seized her. *Screw the gas, she had to get out of there before someone saw her.*

In an instant, she turned and bolted from the store, her heartbeat hammering in time with her footsteps. She fumbled with her car door, yanked it open, and jumped inside. The engine roared to life, tires screeching against the pavement as she sped away, leaving the empty gas station—and the terrifying accusation—behind her.

Simetra's fingers trembled as she clutched the steering wheel, her mind spinning faster than the city lights streaking past her windshield. The gas station was already a distant blur in her rearview mirror, but the news anchor's voice still echoed in her ears, accusing, condemning.

With fumbling hands, she snatched her phone from the passenger seat and pressed the number she knew by heart.

It barely rang before Phyllis picked up.

"Hello? Are you there?" Phyllis's voice was laced with concern.

Simetra swallowed hard, her throat tight, her pulse erratic. "Nevell's dead," she rasped, barely recognizing her own voice. "The police… they think I killed him."

Silence.

Then, Phyllis breathed, sharp and audible. "That's crazy. Where are you?"

"I-I'm in the car. Driving. I need to stop somewhere to figure out what to do."

"Come to me," Phyllis said, urgency replacing shock. "We'll sort this out together. But, Simetra… it might be best to turn yourself in. You know you didn't hurt Nevell."

Simetra's grip tightened around the steering wheel, her knuckles pale in the glow of passing headlights. The world blurred around her, but Phyllis's words rang clear.

"You're right," she whispered. "You're right. I'll go to the police."

"Wait for me at my place first," Phyllis urged. "I'll go with you."

Simetra exhaled. "Okay. I'm on my way."

As she turned down a quieter street, the panic still buzzed beneath her skin, but for the first time since she saw her face on that screen, she didn't feel she was completely alone.

CHAPTER 55

The red glow of the traffic light bathed Simetra's car in an eerie haze. Her fingers tapped anxiously against the steering wheel, her thoughts filled with Phyllis's words.

She would go to the police. Phyllis would be by her side.

But then, out of the darkness, a streak of motion.

Phyllis's SUV barreled through the intersection, speeding past in the wrong direction. Away from her apartment. Away from Simetra.

Simetra's stomach twisted.

Where the hell is she going?

"Phyllis!" she shouted, as if her voice could cut through the night, through the distance between them. Without thinking, Simetra yanked the wheel to the side, making a sharp U-turn. Tires squealed against asphalt as she pressed her foot to the gas, chasing Phyllis down the empty road.

Phyllis was going the wrong way.

And Simetra was about to find out why.

The loading dock behind Mercy Hospital was shrouded in dim orange light, the overhead fluorescents buzzing faintly against the quiet of the late night. Cardboard boxes of scalpels, gloves, and sterile Foley bags lined the dock. Each box was stamped with the familiar insignia of MidTown Medical Supply.

Phyllis's SUV sat idling in the empty loading bay, its taillights glowing like embers in the dark. She moved swiftly, lifting boxes from the dock and stacking them in her trunk with careful precision. There was an urgency to her movements.

The metal door to the hospital slid open, and a worker stepped out, his silhouette momentarily framed by the sterile brightness inside. Without a word, he took the remaining boxes from the dock, disappearing back into the depths of the hospital.

Phyllis pulled her SUV forward, slipping into the shadows just as another Midtown Medical Supply truck appeared. Its logo was smeared with dirt from long-haul miles. It backed into the loading bay, brakes hissing.

Two workers emerged. They wasted no time. Broken IV poles clattered as they were tossed into the truck bed. The mangled remains of hospital beds followed, their dismantled frames stacked without care. Ventilators—gutted and lifeless—were hauled inside, their hollow forms swallowed by the darkness of the truck's interior.

The dock had transformed into a quiet exchange, a routine that spoke of efficiency through continued practice.

Simetra sat in the shadows of the alley. Her car nestled between the brick walls like a silent witness. The dashboard lights cast a dim glow, illuminating the hard lines of her face as she watched the loading dock with unwavering focus. But her attention wasn't on them.

It was on Phyllis.

Phyllis stood by the supply truck, clipboard in hand, her presence as commanding as ever. She barely glanced at the inventory before handing it over.

"All of the damaged items are accounted for," she told the driver, her tone brisk, decisive. "You've got what you need. Now, hurry up and get that truck out of here."

CHAPTER 56

The driver gave a short nod, jumped into his seat, and within seconds, the vehicle growled to life. The taillights flared as the truck rolled out of the loading bay, disappearing down the road.

Phyllis exhaled, prepared to leave—until Simetra stepped out from the alley.

Phyllis froze, her expression unreadable.

"You missed your calling on both previous counts," Simetra said, voice edged with bitter amusement. "You deserve an Academy Award for your acting skills."

Phyllis's eyes hardened.

"Your opinion of me may be shitty right now," she said, measured but firm, "but you don't get to judge me. I did what I had to do."

The air between them thickened, charged with unspoken history, with consequences waiting to unravel.

Simetra wasn't ready to let this go.

Simetra's voice cut through the night, raw with disbelief. "People are dead. Does that even matter to you?"

Phyllis's expression hardened even more.

"I hate it for Mr. Walach and that Ambrose kid," she said, voice steady, but hollow. "But fuck being arrested. I've gotten into bed with people who don't mind killing a bitch." Her lips curled in something that wasn't quite a smile. "I'm in too deep to get out."

Simetra felt the air shift, the weight of those words settling heavy between them. Phyllis had made her choices—terrible, irreversible choices.

Simetra swallowed, her pulse a steady thrum in her ears. "You changed the machine in the Psych Ward, didn't you?"

For the first time, Phyllis's face showed a crack in her carefully constructed armor.

Phyllis barely flinched at Simetra's accusation. Instead, she exhaled, as if she had expected this moment all along.

"I needed some insurance," she admitted, her voice level. "Just in case."

And just like that, the past engulfed Phyllis in a rush of memory.

She is in the Mercy Hospital Maintenance Department. The hospital was silent at this hour, save for the occasional hum of distant machinery. Phyllis moved through the dim corridor, her steps quick but measured. At the back of Maintenance, a rusted metal sign marked **SCRAP** loomed overhead.

She barely hesitated as she reached for the electroshock machine resting on the housekeeper's cleaning cart. Her fingers curled around its worn edges, lifting it with practiced ease.

The smell of burnt plastic lingered in the air, acrid and dense. Phyllis stood in front of the incinerator, its faint heat still emanating from the metal frame.

She reached inside, pulling out what remained of another electroshock machine. The casing was charred to bits. What was left of the wires fused into unrecognizable knots.

Without a word, she wrapped the ruined device in a thick trash bag, cinching it tightly before tucking it under her arm.

CHAPTER 57

Phyllis steps onto the Psych Ward. The fluorescent lights buzzed softly as she moved down the deserted hallway. Every footstep echoed, a whisper of sound in the sterile stillness.

At the entrance to the shock therapy suite, she paused. A quick glance over her shoulder confirmed she was alone.

She slipped inside.

The machine landed on the treatment table with a dull thud. She pushed it as close to the wall as possible, but the cord—severed, useless—dangled just short of the outlet. It didn't matter.

It only needed to look right.

Peeling off her latex gloves, Phyllis tossed them in the nearby bin and hurried from the room, leaving behind the remnants of her deception.

Back in the present, Simetra's stare burned into her.

"You changed the machine in the Psych Ward, didn't you?"

Phyllis didn't answer. But the truth settled between them, undeniable.

When Phyllis finally spoke, her voice was steady, but there was an edge to it. "I didn't think anyone would look close enough to the machine to see that it was different," she admitted. "Or that the cord had been burned off in the incinerator."

Simetra's pulse quickened. "What did you do with the machine that was used on Spencer?"

Phyllis stiffened, her expression unreadable. "I can't tell you that, Doll," she said, her tone quiet but firm. "I still need that machine to keep from ending up dead."

Simetra took a slow step forward, her gaze unwavering. "Well, I need that machine to prove that something was wrong with it," she said, her voice laced with conviction. "The hospital was negligent for allowing it to be used on Spencer."

The words hung between them, charged with weight neither of them could ignore.

Phyllis's jaw tensed. When she spoke again, her voice was cold, unyielding. "Unlike you, Miss High and Mighty, who stands to inherit a fortune, I need this job." She squared her shoulders, her stance defiant. "So pardon me for not wanting to die or get put out on the streets."

The resentment in her voice was sharp enough to cut with.

Simetra inhaled slowly, absorbing the reality of Phyllis's situation. She thought of the impossible choices that had led them to this moment. But she wasn't ready to back down.

Not yet.

Simetra's voice was firm, edged with determination. "We can't just act like nothing happened. We have to go to the police."

For a moment, Phyllis hesitated. Then she nodded. "Alright, I'll go with you. Let's take my car."

"No," Simetra said quickly. "Let's take mine."

Phyllis didn't argue. She followed Simetra to the car, sliding into the passenger seat with practiced ease. The alley was silent, the streetlights casting long shadows over the pavement.

Simetra exhaled, fastening her seatbelt. Her fingers found the key fob, hovering just above the ignition.

That's when the sharp sting of electricity jolted through her body. She never saw the taser that Phyllis hit her with.

A strangled gasp escaped her lips as every muscle in her frame seized. Her vision blurred, the edges tunneling into blackness. The last thing she saw was Phyllis's cold, unflinching stare.

Then—nothing.

Phyllis sighed, shaking her head as she reached for the door handle. "I won't be going to the police with you after all, Doll."

She stepped out into the night, the silence wrapping around her like a cloak. Before she walked away, she glanced back at Simetra's slumped form.

"I'll call someone to let them know where to find you."

With that, she disappeared, leaving Simetra unconscious in the stillness of the alley.

CHAPTER 58

The hospital's maintenance department was so quiet that the hum from the fluorescent lights was deafening. Phyllis moved along carefully to the room designated for SCRAP. Her steps were muffled against the linoleum. It was dark inside the room. Phyllis kept the flashlight low, its narrow beam slicing through the darkness as she wove her way toward the back of the huge space.

The storage area smelled of dust and industrial cleaners. The air was tinged with something stale. Rows of shelves loomed on either side of her, crammed with discarded supplies and forgotten equipment. But Phyllis had only one destination in mind.

She glanced behind her once just to be certain she was alone. Slowly, she eased open the door and slipped inside.

The bins were filled with remnants of past operations, broken instruments, shattered plastic, twisted coils of wiring. Phyllis sifted through them with steady hands, her fingers grazing smooth surfaces, sharp edges. Then she found it. She felt the hairs on the back of her neck raise when she picked up the black plastic bag buried beneath the clutter.

Her breath caught as she peeled it open. The machine lay inside. The same device that had been used on Spencer Walach.

For a moment, she only stared. Then, she tucked it back into the bag and secured it on top of a rolling cart.

Behind her, Phyllis hears an animal growl. She turns to see a huge pit bull with barred teeth. The dog slowly approaches Phyllis. He continues to growl.

Phyllis barely had time to register the shift in the shadows before the tall figure emerged. The glow from the overhead light caught the edges of his mask, highlighting the void where a face should be.

"You only had one job," he said, his voice low, edged with quiet menace. "And you couldn't even do that. You just had to get greedy."

Phyllis swallowed hard but refused to let her fear show. She squared her shoulders. She knows instinctively that things are not going to end well for her.

"It was never about greed, asshole," she shot back. "It was always about survival."

The masked man tilted his head slightly, as if considering her words, then let out a quiet, humorless chuckle.

"You talk about survival," he murmured, stepping forward. "In the afterlife, I'll invite you to let me know how that worked out for you."

Phyllis felt the walls close in, the sterile scent of the hospital mixing with the creeping dread curling at the edges of her mind. There was nowhere to run, no one coming to save her.

And yet she wasn't about to go down without a fight.

She locks eyes with the masked man. Her eyes filled with terror, and his with pure hatred. "Hades, devour," he commands. Hades circles Phyllis, closing the distance between them with each movement.

Phyllis swings the flashlight at the dog and barely misses him. She swings a second time. Hades dodges the blow and lunges for Phyllis.

He hits her full in the chest, knocking her backward. Phyllis falls to the floor, landing on her behind with a thud.

She groans in pain as Hades stands over her.

Phyllis screams. Hades tears at her arms and clothing. The flashlight hits the floor and cracks as the lights go out.

CHAPTER 59

Levi Stone stepped into the hospital storage room in the Maintenance Department. The sharp scent of blood thick in the air. Phyllis lay motionless in the body bag on the floor. The black vinyl was slick with blood.

Levi's breath came short as he crouched, pulling out his phone. The paw prints smeared through the crimson pool made his stomach twist. Images of what could have made the prints swirled around in Levi's brain. *Whatever had left them wasn't human. Whatever animal that did this was pretty damn big.*

He snapped photos of the prints. The shutter's click broke the suffocating silence.

"I don't know what to make of this," Levi muttered, his voice barely above a whisper. "Whoever did this is sick."

The words hung in the room, unanswered.

Officer Greg Shepherd stepped into the maintenance department. The air was thick with the scent of rust and old machinery.

His eyes swept the room filled with rows from floor to ceiling of discarded medical equipment. There are several piles of metal parts earmarked to be scrapped.

Shepherd approached Levi, extending a pair of gloves to him. "I brought you these."

Levi took the gloves, snapping them on with a loud pop.

"I can go with the body if you'd like me to," offered Shepherd.

"No was Levi's response. "Glove up. I don't know what I'm looking for, but a fresh set of eyes may help me find it." Shepherd sighed. *That was just what he needed, to get stuck alone with Levi Stone in the space marked by death.*

Here, in this forgotten corner, something monstrous had left its mark. Shepherd had a sinking feeling it wasn't done yet.

Levi Stone lingered near the doorway, flipping through a report. "Anything sticking out at you?" he asked, his voice low.

Shepherd didn't answer. His focus was drawn to the floor, scattered bloodied paw prints trailing toward a cluster of metal scraps, stopping abruptly where deep gouges cut through the concrete. Something heavy had been dragged here.

He crouched, running his fingers along the marks, feeling the rough edges. Whatever had been here wasn't just moved—it was ripped away. The silence pressed in as he traced the outline of a space where something should have been.

The woman in the body bag had died here. And the killer had left in a hurry.

A sound—a soft scrape against metal. Shepherd's head snapped up. The air had shifted, thick with anticipation.

He followed the sound deeper into the open space. He looked behind boxes and opened closed doors, only to find no one. Shepherd didn't have a good feeling as he walked back into the room with Levi.

Up in the rafters above the rows, someone was watching.

CHAPTER 60

Simetra's head throbbed as consciousness pulled her back into the world. The cold leather beneath her palms. The stench from the mixture of smells in the air grounded her. Garbage and sweaty clothing from the bums in the alley reminded her she was still here. Wherever *here* was.

A dull ache pulsed at the base of her skull as she rubbed it, trying to piece together the last few moments before everything had gone black. Her phone rang, sharp and sudden, shattering the silence.

She gasped, scrambling for it. The name flashing on the screen made her heart jolt.

Cecil.

She fumbled to answer. "Cecil? Is that you?"

His voice crackled through the speaker, frantic.

"Yeah, it's me, Mama. Where the hell are you?"

Simetra blinked hard, trying to focus. The alley stretched in both directions, barely illuminated by the dim glow of a flickering streetlamp. Shadows clung to the brick walls, turning everything into vague, shifting shapes.

She swallowed, gripping the phone tightly. "I think… I'm in one of Nevell's cars," she muttered. The dashboard, the leather seats. It all felt familiar, though that only deepened the unease twisting in her stomach.

Simetra's hands trembled as she pressed the speaker button. Cecil's voice crackled through the small device, sharp and urgent.

"Whatever you do, don't go back to your brother's place—it's crawling with cops."

The weight of his warning settled over her like a cold fog.

"How do you know?" she asked, keeping her voice steady.

"I barely got out of there before they caught me," Cecil responded. "I went there looking for you when I saw your face plastered all over the news."

A sharp gust rattled the alley's trash cans. She forced herself to sit up straighter. "The last thing I remember…" Her breath hitched. "My best friend tased me."

Silence.

Cecil cursed under his breath. "You sure you ain't dreaming?"

Simetra shut her eyes, trying to steady herself against the nausea creeping up. No. This wasn't a dream. It was real—*too* real. And she had no idea what was coming next.

Simetra's pulse pounded in her ears. Phyllis. The one person she never thought would betray her—the one she trusted without hesitation. Her absolute ride or die friend totally flipped the script on her.

She scanned the alley. The shadows seemed thicker now. She could swear she was looking at the silhouette of a man in a ball cap lurking in the darkened corner between the hospital and the alley.

Fear tightened in her chest.

Where the hell was Phyllis?

A sharp wind cut through the narrow space, rattling a loose metal sign. Simetra shivered, more from the weight of realization than the cold. Someone was in the alley with her.

Phyllis had *left* her. Tased her. Dropped her here like an afterthought.

Things didn't add up.

She began to panic. So far, the shadow in the alley hadn't moved… but what if it came towards the car?

 This wasn't the time to fall apart. If Phyllis weren't here, she couldn't stay there alone. She needed to get out—fast.

Simetra spoke into the phone, her breath uneven.

"Where are you now?" she asked.

Cecil's voice came through steady, unfazed.

"Downtown Newport News," he replied.

She swore under her breath. "You do know you could get killed down there."

"I have to admit, I was enjoying kicking it at your place. But right now, downtown is pretty safe. I don't have to worry about cops looking for me here."

Simetra scanned the alley with leery eyes. Every shadow felt like a threat.

"I've got to get off the Peninsula tonight," she said. "I've got to get rid of this car."

There was silence for a beat. Then Cecil's voice came, low and certain.

"Pick me up. We can walk the rail line to Williamsburg. It'll take us about an hour or so. I can get us a room when we get there. Nobody is looking for me."

Simetra didn't hesitate. She thumbed the end call button.

The plan had shifted. And she had no choice but to move now.

CHAPTER 61

Simetra exhaled slowly as she stood in the shadows outside the motel entrance. She couldn't believe her eyes. Right in front of her, a nearly naked woman of the night passed a folded bill to the man. He pocketed it and whispered something into her ear. They walked off together, the man's hand possessively glued to the professional's derriere.

Cecil emerged from the lobby, sticking his head out of the entrance. His fingers twitched slightly—a subtle signal. "Time to move," he muttered under his breath.

Simetra read his lips and stepped out of the shadows, pulling her hood tight over her face. She slid past a haggard man smoking under the buzzing red motel sign. His stare pressing against her back gave her the creeps.

Cecil opened the side door just wide enough for her to slip inside. The motel hallway reeked of stale cigarettes and gungah.

"Don't look at the cameras," he muttered, leading her deeper inside.

Cecil used the key card, and suddenly, he and Simetra were inside. The room was exactly what she expected. It was dim and suffocating. Her mind rushed to formulate scenarios of stories that started here that hadn't ended well.

Her eyes landed on the bed in the middle of the room.

Simetra stepped close to the bed before facing Cecil.

"A motel on the Ho stroll, Cecil? Really?"

Cecil dropped the key card onto the nightstand with a dull thunk.

Cecil tossed his bag on the ratty couch by the door.

"Nobody is going to come looking for you here."

Cecil's smirk was barely visible in the dim glow of the streetlight bleeding through the crack in the curtain.

"Don't worry, Mama, I get it," he said, tossing his jacket onto the couch. *"Anybody that knows you knows the only way you'd be caught in a place like this is if you were dead."*

Simetra let out a dry laugh, crossing the room with careful steps. The chair looked the least contaminated, and right now, comfort was a luxury she wasn't willing to risk.

She pulled it out and dropped into it, arms folded. "I've got dibs on the chair. There's no telling what kind of diseases are breeding in that bed."

Cecil shrugged, already rifling through his bag. "Suit yourself, but don't expect to get any sleep. That chair was designed to aggravate your back."

He emptied the contents onto the couch—a burner phone and a laptop, still smelling faintly of cheap plastic and refurbishment.

"Got you these," Cecil said.

Simetra arched a brow. "How?"

He leaned back, smirking. "Called in a favor, a pawn shop guy owed me."

She stared at the devices, her fingers itching to power them on. She was desperate to connect to something outside the walls of the motel.

Simetra powered on the burner phone and set it on the charger. She did the same with the laptop when, out of the blue, the knock came like a warning shot.

Simetra and Cecil froze. The second knock was harder, impatient. Simetra moved fast, pressing herself into the shadows behind the door. Cecil squared his shoulders, exhaling through his nose before cracking the door open.

A man stood there, leaning too close, eyes darting past Cecil into the room like he had

some right to be there. Cecil wasn't having
it.

"Is there a problem?" he asked, voice
sharpened to a razor's edge.

The guy hesitated, then grinned—an oily,
knowing grin.

"Relax, man. Just wondering if you've got
an extra raincoat for my Jimmy."

Silence stretched, thick and uncomfortable.

Simetra blinked, disbelief knotting tight in
her chest. *You've got to be kidding me.*

Cecil barely reacted, cool as stone.

"Vending machine in the lobby," he said,
voice flat.

The man lingered for a second too long
before finally backing off. Cecil shut the
door, sliding the chain home, double locking
it for good measure.

Simetra exhaled, shaking her head. "Classy
place you picked here, Cecil."

Simetra and Cecil exchanged a glance—a
silent understanding passing between them.
Sleep wasn't in the cards tonight.

"I don't like the way he was trying to see if I was in here alone," Cecil muttered, jaw tight.

Simetra nodded, unease threading into her voice. "His coming to the door this late seemed off to me."

Cecil grabbed the key card and made his way toward the door. His movements were sharp, decisive.

"Don't open this door to anyone, you hear me, Mama? I'm going to take a look around outside. Won't be long."

The door clicked shut behind him, leaving Simetra in heavy silence.

She moved to the window, easing the curtain back just enough to peer into the darkness. Her breath hitched—just for a second— when she thought she saw the shape of a man standing just beyond the reach of the streetlight.

She jerked back instinctively, pulse hammering.

The air in the room tightened around her.

After a moment, she gathered the nerve to check again.

Nothing.

Only empty space.

Had she seen something? Or was the night playing tricks on her?

Her fingers tightened around the curtain's edge as the thought lingered.

CHAPTER 62

Levi leaned back in his chair, flipping through the stack of photos on his desk. The grainy snapshots captured moments of Simetra and Phyllis clinking glasses at an upscale spa.

There were photos of both women wandering around in the halls of the Mariner's Museum, admiring paintings and other marine-inspired artwork.

He turned over one of the pictures, thumb grazing the faded ink scrawled across the back.

NOTE: *Somebody is enjoying her newfound wealth.*

At first sight, Levi assumed the pictures may have been sent by someone jealous of Simetra Thomas. They even had photos of Simetra tooling around town in Mr. Carter's luxury cars.

Thinking a bit deeper, the big picture began to become clearer. Whoever had taken these photos wanted him to know that Simetra Thomas had a reason to kill Nevell Carter.

But that wasn't all. Could they possibly be from the person who killed Mr. Carter? It wouldn't be too far-fetched to suggest that he suspected Ms. Thomas.

But what about the other deaths? They weren't random.

Levi knew that much.

Nevell Carter had been found murdered in his own home. Phyllis Barlowe—ripped apart in a hospital where she should have been safe. Spencer Walach, electrocuted mid-treatment. Justin Ambrose, crushed in an alley like discarded refuse.

The body count wasn't just stacking up—it had long crossed into serial killer territory.

And then there was the note and the photos.

Justin had sent the first one. But Justin was dead.

Which meant someone else had picked up where he left off, leaving breadcrumbs for Levi to follow.

Levi leaned over his desk, studying the case files, the pattern, the thread that connected them all. And there she was at the center.

All of the bread crumbs led to Simetra Thomas.

A woman tangled in the murder of her own brother. She was the common denominator in an equation stained with blood. Now she was missing.

Levi exhaled, rubbing his temples, dread pooling deep in his gut.

What the hell was he going to do now?

Levi leaned against the desk, the weight of the envelope pressing into his palm. His mind raced, piecing together the implications of the pictures inside—grainy, yet unmistakably damning. Someone wanted him to see this. Someone wanted him to know.

He exhaled slowly, bringing his phone to his ear.

It rang twice before a familiar voice answered.

"Where did you get the envelope you put on my desk?" Levi asked, his voice measured but firm.

A pause.

"A woman dropped it off at the front desk," Officer Shepherd on the other line replied, casual, indifferent. He didn't even ask why Stone would call him this late. But then he already knew that Stone had put him on desk duty on purpose tonight.

Levi clenched his jaw. "The drop off should be on the surveillance camera mounted near the entrance," Levi mused aloud. Remembering that he was still on the phone, he cleared his throat. "I'm going to need that footage."

"Alright. It's on the way to you now."

Within minutes, Levi was looking at the footage from the camera on his desktop.

The woman exiting the lobby in the station was tall, her figure shapely, but she wore a wig and kept her face away from the camera.

Levi studied the woman's silhouette visible in the reflection of the glass door. Not much to go on—but it was enough to start.

Another pause.

Levi glanced at his watch. Midnight. There was no time like the present to get it in gear.

He pocketed the envelope, grabbed his keys, and stepped into the night.

CHAPTER 63

The glow of the television flickered across the stained walls, casting restless shadows in the dim motel room. The news anchor's voice droned, crisp yet detached, recounting the latest version of Simetra's flight from the law.

Simetra leaned forward, elbows on her knees, fingers laced tightly together. Every frame—every distorted image of herself running, hiding, a fugitive—chipped away at her resolve.

Beside her, Cecil reclined on the couch, arms crossed. He watched, but didn't comment. Not yet.

Then came Nevell's name.

Simetra sucked in a breath. The footage shifted to a shot inside his bedroom where he'd been found. The image of him on the machines still burned into her mind. The way they spoke about his death made it feel more permanent. More real.

She blamed herself.

If she'd been with him, if she'd seen something, done something…

Her thoughts blurred into static, tangled with grief and guilt.

"Hey," Cecil murmured.

She barely heard him.

"Hey Mama."

She blinked, glancing at him. His gaze was steady, serious.

"You can't do this to yourself."

She swallowed, turning back to the screen.

"I just don't know who could've done this," she whispered.

Silence stretched between them.

Then Cecil shifted forward, resting his elbows on his knees. His voice was quiet, but deliberate.

"You know what we've gotta do, right?"

"Have I told you how much having you here means to me?"

"You don't have to tell me, Mama. I already know. Don't worry, I got you."

Simetra managed a weak smile as she headed toward the door. Cecil jumped up from the couch, falling in step behind her as they took one last look at the motel room.

Outside in the car, the engine coughed to life, sputtering before settling into a reluctant growl. Cecil grinned, giving the dashboard a reassuring pat as he pulled the car away from the cracked pavement onto the street.

Simetra folded her arms, watching the horizon beyond the salvage yard. Rusted machinery leaned like abandoned relics, the smell of oil and dust thick in the air.

She sighed, shaking her head. "How far do you think we're going to get in this hunk of junk?"

Cecil scoffed. "This is not junk. It's a classic." He adjusted the rearview mirror, then smirked. "Besides, it's a loaner. Dude wants this back."

Simetra shot him a look—half disbelief, half exhaustion. "It's going to have to do for now."

Cecil drummed his fingers on the steering wheel.

Simetra's jaw tightened as she glanced at the crumpled paper in her hand.

"What you got there, Mama? A name. A last-known location."

Simetra gave Cecil the eye roll. "I should be so lucky," was her response.

"To find someone who can help us," she murmured.

Cecil nodded, shifting gears. "Then let's make this classic fly."

He pressed the accelerator, and with a reluctant roar, the car lurched forward—to whatever lay ahead.

CHAPTER 64

The afternoon sun streamed through the blinds of Damon O'Neal's office, casting harsh, golden lines across the cluttered desk.

Simetra sat stiffly across from him, hands clenched into fists on her lap, her jaw locked so tight it ached. She had never wanted to be here, but desperation had a way of cornering people.

Damon leaned back in his chair, fingers drumming against the armrest. "How crazy are you?" He let the question settle between them, then leaned forward, his glare cutting straight through her like shards of glass.

"Why would you show up here knowing the cops are looking for you?"

His dark eyes flicked toward the office door like he expected the cops to barge in any second. This time when he spoke, his voice was low but sharp, laced with frustration.

Simetra exhaled slowly through her nose, her breath shaky but controlled. "I'm out of my mind crazy," she said, her voice tight with grief. "My brother is dead. And I need to find out how he died." Her hands curled tighter, nails biting into her palm. "But I've got this teeny tiny obstacle in the way."

"What might that be?" Damon asked.

"I can't get near my brother because the authorities think that I'm a murderer."

The weight of her words filled the space between them, suffocating and raw. Damon studied her, something unreadable flickering across his face—pity, maybe, or calculation.

He sighed, rubbing a hand down his jaw. "Did it occur to you that running from the cops is making you look guilty?"

Simetra's chest tightened at the weight of Damon's accusation. The air in the office seemed to shrink, pressing against her like an invisible force. She swallowed hard, but the bitter taste of disbelief lingered in her throat.

Damon folded his arms, watching her with that infuriatingly detached expression— calm, controlled, unaffected by the storm brewing inside her.

"What do you want from me?" he asked, voice flat.

Simetra leaned forward, her nails digging into the armrest of the chair. "Help me find out who would want to kill Nevell. That's the only way I can prove my innocence."

Damon let out a slow, measured breath, eyes narrowing. "What makes you think I know who might've wanted Nevell dead?" He tilted his head, scrutinizing her in a way that made her skin crawl. "From where I'm sitting, the person with the most to gain from Nevell's death is you."

The words cut through her like a jagged blade. Simetra gasped, shock flashing across her face before it was swallowed by fury. She squared her shoulders, jaw tightening.

"You think I killed my brother?" Her voice trembled—not with fear, but with rage.

"Do you know how insane that sounds?"

Damon didn't flinch. "Doesn't matter how it sounds. It matters what people believe."

Simetra's pulse pounded in her ears. She forced herself to meet Damon's gaze. "You know I would never harm Nevell."

Damon sighed, leaning back in his chair. "That's not what the cops are saying." He reached for a folder on his desk, flipping it open with slow, deliberate movements. "See, here's the thing—the bank's security team contacted me. Showed me evidence that an account was opened in your name." He paused, letting the words sink in. "Funds from the sale of Nevell's stock."

Simetra stiffened. Her fingers curled around the arms of the chair, nails pressing into the worn leather. "That's a damn lie." It was by sheer force that she held herself together. "I've never touched any of Nevell's stocks."

Damon watched her, his silence stretching long enough to make her skin crawl. Then, he closed the folder with a snap. "You're in deep, Simetra. If you want my help, you need to tell me everything."

Her throat tightened. The world was closing in fast, and the only way out was through.

Damon's face hardened. He exhaled sharply, shaking his head.

"That's not all," he said. "This cop, Levi Stone, hauled me down to the station last night. He had some pretty damning evidence against you."

The words hung in the air, thick and heavy. Simetra's breath hitched, but she didn't speak—waiting, bracing for whatever was coming next.

Damon let his mind drift off in memory as he explained to Simetra in a flashback.

He was in Levi Stone's office, sitting across from him in an uncomfortable straight-backed chair. The man's sharp eyes drilled into him like he was trying to dig the truth out of him.

Stone folded his arms. "We've got a problem, Mr. O'Neal." He slid a folder across the desk, tapping the cover twice. "Your girl—Simetra Thomas? I thought she was a nice person, but what I have is evidence of a crime. Ms. Thomas is right in the thick of it."

Damon hesitated, keeping his expression neutral. "I don't see how this involves me."

Stone leaned in, voice dropping. "You should. This evidence makes her look guilty as hell."

"I don't understand," said Damon.

"You're her legal advice. You can't make me believe you didn't know what she was doing with Mr. Carter's finances.

Damon shows the slightest hint of worry. "What are you going to do?"

Levi pulls out his business card and hands it to Damon. "If Simetra Thomas contacts you, call me immediately. This is not a request."

Back to the present in the office, Damon rubbed a hand over his jaw, meeting Simetra's gaze. "Whatever you think is going on, it's worse than you realize."

"It couldn't possibly be." Simetra's bluntness was anything but. Her words cut like a scalpel.

"You're gonna get yourself killed, Simetra," said Damon. His words are equally blunt.

She leaned in, her eyes dark with fury. "Then I'll die knowing the truth."

Damon's footsteps were heavy against the floor, deliberate, like a man walking toward his own fate. He stopped just short of Simetra, his expression carved from stone.

"I can't go to jail," he said, voice tight.

Something sharp flickered through Simetra's eyes—recognition, understanding, then the cold weight of realization crashing down all at once. She didn't wait for confirmation. She didn't need it.

Her pulse surged like a war drum as she spun for the door.

"Simetra—"

But she was already moving, her breath coming fast, her mind racing faster. She shoved past the chair, reaching for the handle, her fingers grazing the cold metal.

Damon lunged—not fast enough.

She ripped the door open, stepping into the corridor, her heart hammering against her ribs.

Whatever truth she had come looking for, she was certain of one thing now.

Damon wasn't going to help her.

CHAPTER 65

Simetra inhaled sharply as she approached the elevator bank.

She pressed the call button. The small circle lit up, but the elevator didn't arrive fast enough to ease her nerves.

Footsteps echoed from the far end of the hallway. She resisted the urge to turn, her pulse beating against her ribs. The elevator chimed, its doors sliding open. A moment of escape. She released the breath and then stepped forward onto the glass elevator.

Below her, Levi burst through the revolving doors, his breath uneven, his steps urgent. The cool, polished lobby of O'Neal & Associates stretched before him, but he barely registered the marble floors or the sleek furniture. He had to reach Simetra.

He rushed toward the nearest elevator, jabbing the button for the 40th floor with more force than necessary. The doors slid shut, his pulse drumming in his ears. As the elevator rose, his eyes drifted forward, drawn by movement across the lobby.

And there she was.

Simetra stood in the glass-enclosed elevator across from him, suspended like a vision between steel and light. Their eyes met—brief, electric, heavy with everything unsaid. Levi's chest tightened. *Don't go. Wait.*

But Simetra's reaction was instant—panic flashing across her face as she stabbed the "Lobby" button, her movements frantic. She wanted out. Levi had seen her. She had to get away.

Their elevators moved in opposite directions, crisscrossing mid-air, separated by steel and glass. Levi's stare was desperate, his silent plea written in the tension of his body: *Stay. Don't run this time.*

Simetra, lips parted, fingers trembling, kept pressing the button as if sheer force could make her descent faster. If only the doors would open soon. She would disappear before he reached her.

Levi slammed his palm against the cold metal railing. *Not this time.*

But fate had different plans. Simetra had a decent head start on him.

Levi's heart sank as he watched Simetra's elevator descend, carrying her away. Panic surged through him. He slammed his palm against the button, willing the machine to halt. As desperation set in, the elevator car stopped. Without hesitation, he darted out as soon as the doors cracked open, catching another elevator just as it made its way down.

Simetra's elevator touched the lobby floor. The instant the doors slid open, she sprang forward, weaving through the late-afternoon crowd. A woman with a stroller rolled into her path. Simetra sidestepped her just in time. A man dragging a suitcase nearly clipped her ankle, but she pushed forward, eyes locked on the revolving doors ahead.

Levi's elevator dropped, inching downward too slowly. His fingers flexed impatiently at his sides. He needed just one more second.

The elevator stopped. The doors parted.

Simetra reached the revolving door first. She pressed through, the glass spinning in its steady rhythm, pulling her into the city's open air. Levi lunged for it a beat too late, slipping into the next section of the rotating entrance.

A woman pushed in from the sidewalk at the same time. Their movements collided, sending each of them whirling past their intended exits. Levi clenched his teeth, forcing himself to wait through another full rotation. He could still catch Simetra.

He had to.

Simetra stood on the sidewalk assessing the flow of cars and foot traffic. Without hesitation, she raised her hand. A yellow cab slowed at the curb, brakes hissing. She yanked open the back door and slid inside, her pulse hammering.

"Just drive," she muttered, barely glancing at the driver.

The tires peeled away from the sidewalk, the cityscape blurring past.

Then, Levi burst through the doors just as the cab rolled away. His breath was heavy, his body tense. His gaze locked onto hers through the rear window.

For a split second, time stretched. Their eyes met—his full of frustration, hers of relief.

And then she was gone.

Levi clenched his jaw, fists balled at his sides as the cab disappeared down the street.

Just like that, she had slipped away, but soon he would bring her to justice.

CHAPTER 66

The tiny room reeked of musty dampness. Sunlight cut through the grimy blinds, casting streaks of gold across the threadbare carpet and peeling wallpaper. The Ho Stroll was quiet this time of day—most business was conducted under the cover of darkness. It was the perfect place for Simetra and Cecil to disappear, if only for a little while.

Simetra lounged in a battered vinyl chair by the rickety table near the door. Tension rolled off her as she squeezed the TV remote clutched in her hand. She flicked through channels searching for news of the cop's progress in their hunt for her. *How had things gotten to this point? She was running from the law, and Nevell was dead.*

Cecil sat on the edge of the lumpy bed, laptop balanced on his knees, fingers moving fast over the keyboard.

Simetra spent countless seconds between looking at the TV screen and Cecil's hunched shoulders on the bed before she caught the concentrated furrow in his brow.

"What are you doing?" she asked, not looking away from the screen.

Cecil didn't glance up. "Trying to find somewhere for us to hold up for a minute." He exhaled, jaw tight. "That cop Levi almost caught you earlier? Had my stomach in knots."

Simetra sighed, pressing the remote down on the table with a sharp click. "Mine too." She stood, crossing the room in quick strides until she dropped onto the mattress beside him, the springs creaking under her weight.

She hesitated, then nodded at the laptop. "Do you mind if I check my email?"

Cecil finally met her gaze, considering. Then he tilted the screen toward her. "I don't see much harm in it. We're leaving out of here anyway—but make it quick."

Simetra pulled the laptop closer, fingers hovering over the keys. Somewhere out there, things were shifting—whether she was ready or not.

Cecil traded places, leaving her on the bed while he grabbed the remote and started flicking through the channels.

Simetra's fingers tapped against the keys with restless energy, navigating to her email inbox.

A bold subject line caught her eye—**APEX BIOTECH INVESTOR INVITATION**. Her pulse quickened as she clicked the message open.

**DEAR INVESTOR,
YOU HAVE BEEN INVITED TO MEET WITH MR. TREVOR KNOX, CEO OF APEX BIOTECH.
MR. KNOX WILL DISCUSS PLANS FOR THE COMPANY'S FUTURE GROWTH ON OCTOBER 10, 2025, AT 7:30 P.M.**

She reread the email twice, the second time aloud for Cecil to hear.

"I wonder what that's all about?" she muttered, more to herself than to Cecil.

Cecil quickly looked up from the TV, shaking his head. "We don't care," he said, voice firm. "This might be the chance we've been waiting for—to get close to the person pulling the strings at Apex."

Simetra glanced at him, raising an eyebrow. "Seems like you're all hyped about this meet and greet."

Cecil leaned forward, resting his elbows on his knees. His expression darkened. "Never that, Mama. Ole Spence was good people. Because of the people at Apex, he's dead. Because of what Nevell knew, you lost your brother." He exhaled sharply. "We have to let everybody know who these people really are."

Simetra leaned back in her chair, hands curling around the laptop's edges. "I don't want to just blow the whistle on them," she said, eyes cold with determination. "I'm going to shut 'em down."

The motel room felt smaller, the walls pressing in as the weight of the words settled. They weren't just running anymore. They were preparing for war.

At that moment, Cecil stopped his channel scrolling when he landed on the news. He sat upright in the chair, muscles stiffening as he watched the image on the screen. "Hey, Mama, I think you better take a look at this."

Simetra gasped aloud as Nevell's nurse appeared onscreen inside Nevell's bedroom.

A female news reporter shoved a mic in her face in front of rolling cameras. Although she was the same nurse Simetra had fired, something about her was different.

The woman looked polished but worn, dark circles beneath her eyes betraying sleepless nights. Simetra turned up the volume.

"I think she killed him," the nurse declared, voice steady, unwavering. "She was living her best life while she left me here every day with Mr. Carter. She started dressing up, going out to parties. Driving around in his cars. I knew all along she decided not to wait to get her piece of the pie."

Simetra couldn't believe what she was hearing. The woman's words stung—not because they were unexpected, but because they were drenched in venom. She could feel Cecil watching her, but she didn't meet his gaze.

Onscreen, the reporter leaned in, eyes sharp, hungry for more. "Was there anyone else in the house with you at any time that evening?"

The nurse hesitated for only a breath. "Ms. Thomas was the last person to see Mr. Carter alive. I was outside his room to give them some privacy. The next thing I know, I'm waking up on the floor, and Mr. Carter is no longer breathing."

Simetra's heart slammed against her ribs. She stood abruptly, needing to move, needing air—but there was nowhere to go. The motel walls felt suffocating. Her scream came from deep within her belly.

"Who is this reporter, and how in the hell is she able to blatantly let this woman slander me?"

Cecil crossed the room and closed the laptop, watching Simetra carefully. "We need to leave. Now!"

Simetra barely heard him. The accusations were out in the world now, spreading like wildfire, painting her guilty before she'd even had a chance to fight back.

CHAPTER 67

Cecil's car looked like a putt-putt at first glance, but it had stallions under the hood as it cut through the humid night like a blade. The headlights sliced open the darkness ahead. The road stretched endlessly before him, a ribbon of asphalt leading them deeper into the South. The glow of the dashboard cast soft shadows across his face. He adjusted his grip on the wheel.

The **WELCOME TO SOUTH CAROLINA** sign loomed ahead, the reflective letters catching the high beams for just a moment before disappearing behind him. Cecil exhaled through his nose, something about crossing state lines always making the journey feel more real.

Beside him, Simetra slept, curled against the passenger seat, the steady rhythm of her breathing the only sound aside from the hum of the tires. He glanced at her for a brief moment—her features relaxed, her body sinking into the quiet comfort of sleep. His fingers briefly brushed over the top of his braided man bun, adjusting it absentmindedly.

As the miles slipped by, Cecil let himself settle into the drive, the road ahead unwinding like the coils of a huge snake.

God only knew what they were going to find once they got to their destination. To say Cecil had a bad feeling was putting it mildly.

He had a nervous breakdown and washed out of Quantico. The memory pressed against the back of his mind—flashes of dark rooms, unreadable faces, the slow unraveling of everything he thought he was. He hadn't broken under pressure; he had shattered, his mind buckling under the weight of secrets too heavy for any recruit.

They marked him an enemy, a liability, a ghost best left unseen. Cecil walked away from his life as a professional hacker and settled for living undercover on the streets. He never wanted to be discovered again, but somebody killed Ole Spence, and who would look out for Simetra? She'd been kind to him and didn't shun him like he was a dirty pariah.

For her sake, he had to come up with a plan. Simetra was in over her head, tangled in something deeper, darker than she realized.

If he didn't act fast, she could be the next one dead.

"Not on my watch," Cecil muttered under his breath, barely above a whisper.

From the shadowed passenger seat, Simetra stirred. "What are you carrying on about?" she murmured, voice thick with sleep but edged with curiosity.

Cecil kept his eyes on the road, jaw tightening. He could lie—pretend everything was fine, pretend they were just two drifters moving through the night.

But lying had never saved anyone.

"Do you have any idea what you're going to say to this Knox guy when you finally come face-to-face?"

Cecil flicked his eyes off the road for half a second, searching Simetra's expression in the fleeting glow of passing highway lights. Her jaw was tight, her posture rigid—she wasn't just uneasy, she was bracing for something.

"Screw talk," she muttered, voice laced with something cold and raw. "I know what I'd *like* to do, but it's against the law."

Cecil let out a dry chuckle. "Speaking of the law—that Stone guy? He's like a damn bloodhound, and he's got his sights locked on you."

Simetra sighed, rubbing a hand over her face, exhaustion creeping in. "Which is exactly why we need to find Trevor Knox," she said, voice steady, resolved. "And figure out what he knows—before Stone does."

Simetra smiled at Cecil, but there was something unreadable behind it—something that didn't quite reach her eyes.

"First, we have to take care of something very important," she said, her voice quiet but firm.

Cecil's fingers flexed against the wheel. He knew that tone. He knew that whatever came next wouldn't be simple or easy.

The road stretched ahead, dark and uncertain.

Whatever this was, it was about to change everything.

The first streaks of sunrise spilled across the sky as Cecil and Simetra pulled into town, the quiet streets just beginning to stir. The drive had been long, but the weight in

Cecil's chest told him the real journey was only starting.

They entered a thrift store, its worn sign barely catching the morning light. Inside, dust motes danced in the beams streaming through the windows, the scent of aged fabric and forgotten lives lingering in the air.

Simetra moved through the racks, fingers trailing over the fabric. Then she paused, eyes locking onto something buried between faded blouses and old coats—a prom dress, slightly worn, but still the bright shimmer that had not been dulled by time.

She lifted it from the rack, holding it against herself, assessing it.

Cecil glanced at her, his brow furrowing. "Pretty fancy threads, Mama. You're not looking to get chosen by some billionaire bigwig, are you?"

Simetra smirked, but there was something softer behind it. "You never know."

CHAPTER 68

The hum of conversation filled the air as Simetra stepped into the conference room, a space buzzing with sharp suits and quiet deals. Men clustered near the buffet, loading plates with delicate hors d'oeuvres, while waiters moved with practiced efficiency, filling water glasses on elegantly dressed tables.

At the entrance, a polished table held name badges, carefully arranged in neat rows. Two young women manned the station, greeting attendees with professional smiles and hushed tones.

Simetra approached, scanning the names, when the soft but deliberate sound of footsteps behind her made the hairs on her neck rise.

She turned.

Devona Drummond stood before her, smiling—too polished, too knowing.

Simetra stiffened, instinctively bracing. She hadn't expected *this*.

"Looks like you weren't expecting to see me here," Devona said, amusement flickering in her eyes.

Simetra held her gaze, refusing to flinch. "Actually, you were the last person I expected to see here."

Devona's smirk deepened, the energy between them charged, unspoken.

Simetra exhaled slowly. "The invitation said this was a celebration of alumni and a welcome to new investors."

She presented Devona with a hard stare. "I'm new," the voice was lethal.

Simetra picked up her name badge, fingers tightening around the laminated card before slipping it onto her dress. She followed Devona out of the queue, weaving past other attendees, the hum of polite conversation fading as they moved farther from the crowd.

Once they were out of earshot, Simetra grabbed Devona's arm, pulling her off to the side, her voice low but sharp.

"You ought to be ashamed of yourself," she said, eyes blazing. "You're buying products from this guy knowing they were involved in someone's death. What kind of person does that?"

Devona barely flinched. Instead, she exhaled with practiced ease, adjusting the cuff of her sleeve like they were discussing something as trivial as a business deal.

"It's nothing personal," she said smoothly. "It's about business. There's a hefty profit in selling refurbished supplies."

Simetra stared at her, disbelief tightening her throat. How could she be so detached, so calculated?

"That profit has no value if people's lives are at stake," she shot back, voice harder now. "I can't understand how you could be so—so *evil*."

Devona's gaze remained unreadable, but there was something lurking beneath it—a flicker of amusement, maybe even condescension.

"That's the difference between us," she murmured, tilting her head ever so slightly. "You think the world runs on principles. I know for a fact it runs on power."

Devona folded her arms, tilting her head slightly, a slow smirk curling at the corner of her mouth. "You know what your problem is?" she said, voice smooth, practiced. "You ask too many questions."

Simetra didn't move, her stance firm, unyielding.

"You started digging into patients being billed for supplies they never received," Devona continued, the amusement flickering in her tone like a challenge. "You think that's some scandal? Happens every day."

Simetra's expression hardened. "I don't like seeing anyone being taken advantage of."

Devona sighed, shaking her head as if she was explaining something painfully obvious. "It can't be helped. The average person doesn't read their bill—they just trust their insurance company to cover it. An extra Ambu bag here, a few IV lines there. Nobody's keeping track of how many needles or catheters are actually used."

Simetra inhaled sharply, the confirmation hitting like a slap. "So, I was right," she said, her voice low but edged with fire. "The patient charges were being padded."

Devona held her gaze, unbothered, unmoved. She shrugged. "Bingo."

Simetra's breath hitched. "If that wasn't bad enough, you started asking questions about patients being charged for supplies that had been used on other patients after they'd been recalled or scrapped."

Her voice was steady, but her pulse pounded in her ears.

Devona tilted her head, watching her like she was amused.

"How could I not," Simetra continued, her fingers curling into fists at her sides, "when you didn't even *try* to change the serial numbers?" She paused, inhaling sharply, trying to steady the fire rising in her chest. Then, her voice dropped lower, colder. "You're *not* getting away with this."

Devona's smirk barely wavered. "My dear," she said smoothly, "we already have."

Simetra swallowed down the frustration clawing at her throat. She scanned Devona's face, searching for a crack in her confidence, any sign of doubt—but there was none.

"I guess you're here to trick some unsuspecting person into investing," Simetra said, eyes narrowing. "Is that what you did to Nevell?"

Devona gave a slow nod, as if Simetra had finally caught up. "You catch on quick," she mused. "Too bad your brother never did— *even until his last breath.*"

A sharp, involuntary gasp escaped Simetra. Her body went rigid, her vision narrowing on Devona's unreadable expression.

"What do you even know about Nevell?" Simetra's voice was raw now, laced with danger.

Devona chuckled—a sound so indifferent, so devoid of guilt, that Simetra's nails dug into her palms.

"I know Nevell was a loose end," Devona said coolly. "Not to mention, he had enough information from Spencer Walach to shut our operation down."

Simetra's throat tightened. A scream built in her chest, but she swallowed it down, forcing herself to stay in control.

Her jaw clenched.

Her fingers trembled at her sides.

Through gritted teeth, she spoke.

Simetra's breath was unsteady, fists clenched at her sides. "Did you kill Nevell?"

Devona tilted her head, smirking like the question amused her. "What if I did?" she mused, her voice laced with venom. "If I were you, I wouldn't waste time worrying about *me* killing Nevell." She took a slow step forward. "Because I gave the police enough information to pin his murder on *you*."

Simetra's pulse pounded in her ears. "You are a damn monster," she spat, her voice trembling with fury. "It didn't matter to you at all that he was my only living blood relative?"

Devona didn't flinch.

Simetra did.

She moved fast, closing the space between them, the fire in her chest surging. Devona reacted, using her height, swinging—wild, reckless.

Simetra sidestepped.

A second later, her fingers found a fistful of Devona's fake hair.

"I'll teach you the value of blood, bitch!" Simetra snarled as she gave Devona's head a sharp yank, then let go just as quickly.

Devona stumbled, struggling to regain her balance.

Simetra didn't wait—she caught her slipping and struck, landing a sharp left jab, followed by a right punch, remembering what Nevell had taught her.

Devona crumpled.

Out cold.

Simetra exhaled, shaking off the adrenaline still rushing through her veins. She glanced down at Devona's limp form and huffed.

"Oh yeah," she murmured. "Now you know I'm ambidextrous."

CHAPTER 69

Trevor Knox stood at the podium, the weight of his billion-dollar empire resting in the confidence of his stance. The banquet room hummed with quiet conversation, the soft clatter of silverware against porcelain underscoring the murmurs of thirty-something investors, executives, and opportunists—all here to listen, to judge, to decide.

From behind the podium, Trevor took a slow, deliberate breath, letting the moment settle before he spoke.

"From that lengthy introduction, you know all about me," he said, his voice steady, practiced. "You know about my multi-billion-dollar company. I say that it's *my* company—but tonight, I'd like to allow you to say that it's *yours* too."

He let the words hang, scanning the room, watching for the subtle shifts in expression—the flicker of intrigue, the calculation of possibility.

"My goal every morning," he continued, "is to figure out how to get the products we manufacture at Apex and her sister companies into every medical and healthcare facility that spans the globe."

A murmur rippled through the audience—soft discussions, quiet calculations.

Trevor reached for the water bottle on the podium, taking a measured sip before setting it down. He didn't rush. He knew how to hold a room.

Then, with a swift motion, he queued up the slides behind him.

The presentation flashed to life, numbers, projections, possibilities unfolding across the screen.

Now came the moment that mattered.

Would they buy into the vision?

Would they see the opportunity—or the risk?

Trevor already knew his answer.

The real question was—did they?

Trevor Knox stood at the podium, radiating the confidence of a man who had built an empire. His voice carried through the banquet room with ease, his words carefully crafted, rehearsed, and persuasive.

"Over the last quarter, sales have increased over 60% from where they were last year," he announced. "But we're not just about selling product—we're a *community* of investors. And joining that community? That'll only cost you **$500,000**."

A ripple of coughs and throat-clearing traveled through the room. Even the wealthiest in attendance shifted in their seats.

Trevor chuckled, holding up a hand in mock reassurance. "You don't have to pay *all* of it today," he said, a teasing edge to his tone. "We have a payment plan for those who choose to go that route."

The murmurs in the crowd settled as he pressed forward. "Now, I'll jump right into our Pinnacle Celebration. We hold it once a year, and if you join today, you'll become an *alumnus*. What that means is simple—our Alumni attend the Pinnacle and are asked to invite at least *one* guest to celebrate our community. And if your guest joins?" He paused, scanning the faces in the crowd. "You receive financial compensation, as a token of our appreciation for your efforts in growing our community of investors."

Trevor's gaze swept the room, carefully assessing reactions.

Then, the doors swung open.

Simetra burst in, scanning for an empty seat, her pulse still racing from her showdown with Devona in the hallway. She barely spared a glance at the podium—her focus was on blending in, slipping into the background, catching her breath.

But then—

That voice.

She'd heard it before.

Simetra stiffened.

Slowly, her gaze lifted, locking onto the man speaking.

Her stomach twisted.

She knew that face.

Knew it *too well.*

Simetra's breath hitched as her gaze locked onto Trevor Knox.

He was a dead ringer for Scott Colton.

"Dear God," she whispered, barely audible, "there are two of them."

Trevor Knox was staring straight at her.

Her throat tightened.

She dropped her gaze, forcing herself to breathe as he continued his speech, unfazed, unreadable.

Slowly, she pushed herself up from her chair.

Her steps were measured, but her body screamed at her to move faster.

She slipped toward the **EXIT**, her mind racing faster than her feet.

She didn't know what she was walking into.

But she knew what she was running from.

Simetra's breath came fast and sharp as she scanned the hallway, eyes darting for an exit, her pulse hammering like a war drum. Every muscle in her body screamed **move**, but she forced herself to stay composed, just long enough to locate the way out.

Then, there it was—the entrance.

She bolted.

Cecil's jalopy rattled as it pulled up to the front of the hotel, the engine coughing out a strained protest. He barely had time to shift gears before Simetra burst through the entrance like a live wire, sprinting toward the car.

She didn't hesitate—didn't look back.

She yanked open the door and threw herself into the front seat, breathless, voice urgent.

"Get us out of here! Now!"

Cecil didn't ask questions.

He punched the gas.

The tires screeched against the pavement as they tore away from the hotel, the building shrinking in the rearview mirror, swallowed by the night.

CHAPTER 70

Devona stirred, a groan slipping past her lips as her senses fought to catch up. A hand—firm, deliberate—patted her cheek, coaxing her back to consciousness.

"Come on, baby," Trevor murmured, his tone almost tender. "Wake up."

Her fingers instinctively pressed against her temple, searching for blood. None. Just pain. Deep, throbbing, disorienting. The room swam in a haze, shapes blurring at the edges.

"Ah—my head," she muttered, voice raw.

Trevor leaned back, watching her with amusement, as though this was all part of some grand, predictable game. "You just got your lights punched out," he said, the smirk audible in his tone. "By our little office manager. Imagine she came all this way just to bring me into account."

"She was surprised as hell to see me here," said Devona. She didn't bring the police with her. It's obvious she's just fishing for evidence."

Devona blinked hard, trying to ground herself. It took too much time to focus.

Trevor exhaled, shaking his head. "She's got guts," he mused, eyes gleaming with something unreadable. "I have to give her that."

Devona pulled a bottle of water from the small refrigerator. She took a swallow before facing Trevor. Her eyes gleamed with barely contained contempt. "What she's got is a death wish," she spat, voice dripping venom. "That goody two-shoes has been a thorn in my flesh from the very beginning. I can't wait to see her in a cage."

Her gaze flicked to Hades, the black-coated pit sitting at attention in his kennel. The dog's unwavering stare settled on Devona, unreadable but deliberate, as if it saw through her. Devona scoffed.

"She made work difficult, always going over the patient's bill with a fine-toothed comb. She always stuck her nose into the invoices of supplies I ordered. I hated the sight of her. She was the only person I knew who, with a look, could make me feel like trash."

"You should've seen her face when she saw me. That fear in her eyes—" Trevor let out a low chuckle, shifting against the table beside him. "I have to admit, it made my dick hard. Just like now."

He pulled Devona into his arms, allowing no room for escape.

"Perve," Devona snapped. Her disgust curled her lip, but it was hard to tell if she was truly repulsed or simply keeping up appearances.

Trevor's response was swift and unrelenting. His hands wrapped around her throat, tightly, too tightly. Her nails scraped at his skin in protest. He leaned in, breath hot against her ear. "You know you like it rough."

Her struggle was brief but sharp. She broke free, stumbling back, coughing as she dragged air into her lungs. Her fingers traced the red marks blooming on her skin.

"Not that rough," she hissed. "I hope you don't think a stunt like that is going to get you some."

"I had hoped it would," Trevor's voice crackled with need.

Devona shook her head in disbelief.

"You're better off trying your luck with Miss Goody Two-Shoes Simetra."

Trevor seemed to consider the idea. "I wonder what would happen if we were to meet?

Devona rolled her eyes and huffed.

Trevor continued to smirk.

Silence lingered between them like smoke after a fire, dense and suffocating. Hades let out a low, warning growl—a sound that they both heard, but neither of them acknowledged.

Devona paced the length of the room, her heels clicking against the carpeted floor. "Do you think she'll show up at the Pinnacle celebration?" she asked, voice sharp with suspicion.

Trevor leaned back in his chair, casual, smug. "I'm counting on it," he said, swirling the amber liquid in his glass. "I made sure to send her a special invitation to sit at one of the top-tier tables."

Devona stopped in her tracks, turning on her heel. "Why would you do that?" she hissed. Her disbelief quickly spiraled into rage.

"She's not a member. Her invitation was for Nevell, and he's dead."

Devona's fingers curled into fists at her sides, nails pressing deep into her palm. The mere thought of Simetra sent a fresh wave of fury through her. "When I see her again, I'm going to teach her a lesson for laying hands on me," she seethed.

Trevor leaned back against the bar, watching her with a slow, easy smirk. "Easy, girl," he said, tilting his head. "Now you're starting to sound like your old self again. You had me worried."

Her jaw tightened. "Old self." The phrase scraped against her like a dull blade. She had fought—clawed—to become something more, something untouchable. And yet here she was, blood hot, vision sharp, ready to strike like she always had.

Devona exhaled through her nose, steadying herself. "She's a mistake that needs correcting," she muttered.

Trevor chuckled, swirling his drink lazily. "Then let's make sure you don't get sloppy," he said

Devona didn't respond, but the fire in her eyes spoke volumes.

Trevor took a slow sip, savoring the moment. He set his glass down with deliberate care. "She's walking into a world where she doesn't belong, thinking she has some claim over what her brother left behind. I want to see how far she's willing to play this game."

Devona's nails bit into her palm. "She doesn't get to replace Nevell," she snapped.

"Nevell's gone, but his investments are still here," said Trevor, calmly. "For right now, she is the one thing standing between us and Nevell Carter's investments."

"What do you think she'll do?" Devona was already plotting in her mind.

Trevor tilted his head, studying her, a glint of amusement in his gaze. " I don't think we'll have to wait too long before our little office manager makes this a show worth watching."

CHAPTER 71

Inside the police station, Levi Stone sat stiffly in the metal chair, his gaze fixed on the federal agent across from him. Between them, an evidence box held the last remnants of Phyllis Barlowe's life—what was left in her desk at the hospital.

Levi exhaled, rubbing his temple before speaking. "I'm glad to have you guys aboard. I have to admit, I wanted to put an end to these so-called 'accidental deaths,' but even I had to ask for help."

The agent leaned back, arms crossed. "Next time, don't wait so long to get us involved."

The weight of his words settled between them as Levi reached into the box, fingers searching through the contents. A sweater, a wristwatch, and scattered papers. Then his hand closed around something cold and metallic.

A key.

He turned it over in his palm, studying it. Not a house key. Not to a car. Something else.

Levi lifted his eyes to the agent. "Can you find out what this key fits?"

The agent took the key, inspecting it closely. "Looks like a storage lock. I'll get somebody on it right away."

Levi nodded, his jaw tightening. Whatever was behind that lock, it was a piece of a puzzle he wasn't ready to leave unsolved.

The metal door groaned as Levi turned the key, its resistance giving way with a reluctant click. He exchanged a glance with the federal agent before pushing the door open, revealing the dimly lit interior of the storage unit.

Dust floated in the streaks of daylight spilling through the cracks, settling over rows of medical supplies lining the walls. In the middle of the floor, a few crates stood stacked, orderly, almost deliberate.

Near the entrance, two suitcases sat untouched, their presence stark against the industrial concrete. Levi's gaze flicked over them before landing on a table beside them.

He stepped forward, his movements carefully measured. A plain envelope rested on the scratched surface, the weight of its contents revealed as he picked it up. Cash. Thick stacks, crisp and unmarked.

Beside it, several credit cards lay in a neat row. A passport sat next to them—no dust, no wear, almost new.

Levi exhaled slowly, fingers tightening around the envelope as the implications of what they'd found settled in.

Levi let the envelope slip back onto the table, his gaze lingering on the passport and the crisp stacks of cash. "Looks like Ms. Barlowe was planning on taking a trip," he muttered, his voice edged with suspicion.

The agent didn't respond. Instead, he pulled out his phone, his movements brisk, deliberate. He stepped away, pressing the device to his ear.

"Get the team over to the storage unit," he said, low but urgent. "I need to find out everyone who's touched the contents." He paced a short distance, eyes sweeping over the scattered medical supplies, the suitcases, the unsettling remnants of a plan gone unfinished. "This stuff looks like it belonged at the hospital where Ms. Barlowe worked," he continued. "I need to find out why these items are sitting in this woman's personal storage unit."

A pause. The quiet crackle of a response on the other end.

The agent clicked off the line and turned back to Levi. His expression was unreadable, but his posture had shifted—more rigid, more alert.

Something about this wasn't right. And Levi had the distinct feeling they were only scratching the surface.

Levi raised his phone, the screen casting a faint glow in the dim storage unit. He snapped photos of the medical supplies stacked against the walls, then switched to video mode, carefully panning across the space. Every detail mattered—the suitcases, the abandoned machines, the sterile tools that felt out of place in this setting.

His movement slowed as he reached the far end of the unit. A blanket lay draped over something bulky. Frayed edges, dust settling along its folds, as if it had been hastily covered. Levi narrowed his eyes and pulled it back.

Beneath it, the machine was blackened, its surface scarred by heat damage. An electroshock device—but unlike any he'd seen in working condition.

"Well, well…" His voice was quiet, edged with realization. "What do we have here?"

The agent stepped closer, gaze sharp. "Is there some significance to this piece of equipment?"

Levi let out a slow breath, nodding. "I'm beginning to think so. The hospital administrator refused to investigate a case where one of the patients was electrocuted. No body. No machine. Therefore, no crime."

He lifted his phone again, the camera shutter clicking as he documented the charred remains.

He'd discovered a suspicious machine. And Levi had a feeling it wasn't the only secret buried in this storage unit.

Levi studied the charred electroshock machine, the scorched metal speaking to a history no one had wanted uncovered. He exhaled, the weight of the discovery settled deep in his chest.

"Well," he murmured, snapping another picture. "Looks like we may have found the machine that can solve our crime."

The agent's gaze hardened, his phone still gripped in his hand, the call already made for the team to arrive. "Let's hope it's enough," he said, eyes sweeping over the unit. "Because someone went to a lot of trouble to make sure this machine disappeared from the crime scene."

Levi didn't respond immediately. Instead, he zoomed the camera on his phone over the machine's damaged surface. He carefully recorded the rough patches where fire or force had tried to erase the evidence. But evidence had a way of surviving, even when people tried to bury it.

And this? This was a piece of the truth clawing its way back to light.

CHAPTER 72

The hotel suite was bathed in dim light, the air thick with the sharp scent of liquor.

Scott Colton sat on the edge of the bed, rolling the glass between his fingers, watching the ice slowly melt. Across the room, Trevor Knox lounged on the sofa, his posture deceptively relaxed, his own drink cradled in his hand.

Scott let out a low chuckle, shaking his head. "You've really made a mess of things this time, little brother."

Trevor took a slow sip before responding. "I can't take responsibility for all of the blame." He set his glass down, running a hand through his hair. "Your kills were pretty messy, too. You should have known that Benyon woman's body would be found in the lake right away."

Scott's eyes darkened as he leaned forward, his voice dropping to something colder. "You're one to talk. I had to kill Spencer Walach a second time because you couldn't get it done."

Trevor said nothing.

Scott swirled his drink, staring into the liquid, the weight of unfinished business hanging between them. "If that electroshock treatment had actually helped him regain his memory…" he mused, more to himself than to Trevor.

But it didn't. And now, here we are.

Trevor swirled the last of his vodka in the glass, mimicking his twin's hand movement. "He would have definitely gone to the authorities," he muttered, the thought lingering between him and his twin like the taste of their shared liquor.

Trevor smirked, setting his glass down with a quiet clink. "Score one for both of us not being suspected of killing the housekeeper," he said casually, stretching his legs out. "And that nosy electrician who tried to warn Simetra Thomas."

Scott exhaled, shaking his head. There was no pride in their work—just necessity. Loose ends needed cutting, and they had done what needed to be done.

But deep down, Scott knew. Every time they cleaned up a mess, another waited just around the corner.

And sooner or later, one of them wouldn't be able to clean it up.

Scott's grip tightened around his glass, his pulse drumming in his ears. The dim hotel room blurred for a fraction of a second as a memory clawed its way to the surface— sharp, sudden, and undeniable.

A flash of white. He remembered the soft sound of wheels rolling across linoleum.

In his mind, he pictured the housekeeper.

She pushed her cart into the electroshock suite, moving with the steady, practiced rhythm of someone going through routine motions. But Scott saw it now—what he hadn't fully processed before. The way her hands lingered over the machine. The calculated pause before she lifted it onto her cart.

Then it was gone.

The present rushed back, the memory dissolving like vapor. Scott exhaled slowly, his gaze flickering toward Trevor. His brother had no idea what was storming through his mind, but Scott did.

The housekeeper hadn't just been cleaning. She had been an accomplice.

And now, she was dead.

Scott's breath grew shallow, his grip tightening around the glass. The vodka burned as he swallowed, but it wasn't the liquor making his pulse spike—it was the flashes, clawing at the edges of his mind, forcing their way in.

A masked figure.

A taser crackling in the dim light.

Justin Ambrose convulsed as the current ripped through him, his body hitting the floor in a graceless heap.

Carla stood paralyzed. *Why hadn't the machine fired?* Confusion flickered in her wide eyes—until the jolt sent her stumbling forward, her hand slamming down on the switch.

Scott blinked hard.

His own hand had gripped the taser.

His own steps had been calculated, precise.

And Ray Stewart—his final loose end—had been dealt with the same way. No witnesses. No threats.

Scott inhaled slowly, grounding himself in the present, in the dim hotel suite, with the glass sweating between his fingers.

He reveled in the fact that Trevor had noticed the shift in him, the momentary unraveling. That was good.

Scott was thoroughly satisfied that his brother knew just how much of the blood was on his hands.

Scott and Trevor lifted their glasses in unison, the vodka burning its way down, smooth but biting.

Trevor leaned back, exhaling slowly. "At least they won't be looking for either of us for Nevell Carter's death," he mused, swirling the liquor in his glass. "I think it's pretty apropos that his sister is suspect number one."

That hateful woman was always giving me pushback and opposition from the moment I took over as hospital administrator," said Scott, his voice teetering on rage. "There were so many days I wanted to shit can her ass for challenging me in front of other employees."

Trevor's smirk faded, his tone sharpening. "Simetra Thomas is a loose end just like her brother," he continued, setting his glass down with deliberate precision. "If we're going to make it through this debacle unscathed, we have to tie up all our loose ends."

Scott turned the thought over in his mind, the meaning clear, unmistakable.

They weren't done yet.

Not by a long shot.

Scott pushed himself off the bed. He crossed the room, sinking onto the sofa beside his twin. The resemblance between them was uncanny—unnerving, even. Same sharp jawline, same piercing gaze, same quiet danger lurking beneath their polished exterior.

Without a word, the two of them lifted their glasses, the quiet clink ringing through the dim hotel suite like a pact sealed in vodka and blood.

Trevor swirled his drink, eyes gleaming with dark certainty. "I know exactly where to start."

Scott took a slow sip, letting the liquor burn, waiting.

Whatever his brother had in mind, it wouldn't be clean.

But it would be effective.

CHAPTER 73

Trevor stood at the window in his office at APEX BIOTECH. His gaze locked on the darkness beyond the glass. The city stretched before him—lights flickering, streets buzzing with life in the shadows. At his feet, Hades, his massive pit bull, sat still as a statue, muscles coiled with quiet discipline.

Behind him, Devona perched on the edge of his desk, her presence unwavering. Her voice cut through the silence, sharp with conviction. "The more I think about it, the more I'm convinced—we can't let that Thomas woman get away after what she's done."

Trevor didn't turn. His grip tightened subtly over Hades' broad head, fingers trailing over the dog's thick fur. When he finally spoke, his voice was low, measured. "Whatever happens to Simetra Thomas is the least of my worries right now."

A flicker of frustration crossed Devona's face, but she didn't back down. She leaned forward slightly, eyes steady. "Well, she's a loose end that needs to be dealt with."

The weight of her words lingered in the air, curling through the dimly lit office. Trevor exhaled slowly, watching the city shift before him. He wasn't interested in cleaning up past mistakes.

But loose ends had a way of tightening when left unattended.

Devona hesitated before inching closer, her arms sliding gently around Trevor's waist from behind. She felt the warmth of his body beneath the fabric of his shirt, the quiet comfort of contact. But that comfort was short-lived.

A low, rumbling growl cut through the silence.

Hades.

The dog's hackles bristled, his deep-set eyes locked on her with suspicion. His protective stance was unwavering, his body coiled like a loaded spring.

Devona sighed. *Of course.* She had barely touched Trevor, and already the beast had judged her guilty.

"Can't you put Hades in his kennel?" she murmured, keeping her voice calm but firm. "You know how he takes all my movements toward you as a threat. I don't want to get mauled."

Trevor chuckled, though he didn't pull away from her touch. "Don't worry about Hades." He reached down, giving the dog a reassuring pat on the head. "You can't help but admire his loyalty."

Loyalty. Devona knew it was meant as a compliment, but the word twisted inside her chest like something heavier. She swallowed, loosening her hold ever so slightly. The growl faded into a watchful silence, but the tension remained.

Devona paced near the window, arms folded, her gaze distant. "It's been days and we haven't heard a peep out of our Simetra. That witch is planning something, I can feel it."

Trevor sat back, watching her with a measured look. "You may be right." He exhaled, rubbing his jaw. "I can clearly see her going to the authorities and having this place crawling with feds."

Devona huffed, turning on her heel. "Exactly."

"We need to pack up shop and lay low for a while," she said, her voice clipped with certainty. "We can keep our Pinnacle celebration on schedule, just make it virtual. Investors enter by invitation only, pre-registering ahead of time."

Trevor tilted his head, considering. "Not a bad idea," he admitted, but there was a lack of enthusiasm in his tone. A trace of boredom. "But what's the fun in that? The investors really look forward to partying together after the ceremony."

Devona pressed her lips together. He had a point. The energy, the money—it was always better in person. But with Simetra lurking in the background like a shadow, they didn't have the luxury of indulgence.

She narrowed her eyes. "I would love to say let's make it work. Let's adapt. But I got a bad feeling about this one, baby."

Trevor smirked, a flicker of amusement in his gaze. "You always do. But I'll humor you this time. We should lay low out of the country for a while."

Devona's thoughts narrowed to one goal—escape. Simetra Thomas would be handled in due time, but for now, she needed distance. Needed freedom.

She cast a swift glance around the room, scanning for her purse. The moment she spotted it resting on the chair, she freed herself from Trevor's grasp, snatched the bag, and slung it over her shoulder in one fluid motion.

"You ain't said nothing but a word." Her voice was steady, but adrenaline hummed beneath it. She didn't bother asking *why*— only *where*.

Trevor's lips curled into a knowing smirk. "You sure you're ready for this?"

Devona met his gaze without flinching. "I was ready yesterday."

A silent beat stretched between them. Hades gave an approving snort, and just like that, Trevor was on his feet.

"Let's move."

CHAPTER 74

Trevor strode toward the door with deliberate steps.

"Hades, come." His voice was steady, cold.

Without hesitation, the massive form of Hades moved, his dark eyes gleaming as he obeyed. He positioned himself between Devona and the exit, a silent wall of muscle and authority.

Devona's brow furrowed, confusion overtaking her features as she took a hesitant step forward. "Baby, what's going on here?" Her voice was a soft plea, edged with unease.

Trevor inhaled deeply, tilting his head slightly before meeting her gaze with unwavering certainty. "Unfortunately for you, baby, we won't be leaving here together." His words cut through the air, crisp and final. "This is where our partnership ends."

The room grew heavier, thick with tension as realization dawned on Devona. The familiar warmth that once lingered between them had dissipated, replaced by the chilling certainty that Trevor's words were no bluff.

Devona lunged forward, her heels skidding against the floor as she desperately tried to bridge the space between her and Trevor. Her heart pounded, frantic, as the walls seemed to close in around her.

"Hades hold!" Trevor commanded.

A low, guttural growl reverberated through the room. Hades, ever-loyal, lightly squeezed Devona's wrist in his mouth. He sat right in front of Devona, his massive frame radiating a silent warning. The sound rumbled deep in his throat—a predator's promise of protection.

"I know what you're thinking, but you're wrong," Devona pleaded, her voice laced with urgency. "I would never betray you." She dared not move from Hades' grasp.

Trevor let out a harsh breath, his jaw tightening until his words spilled through clenched teeth. "Foolish woman. You invited Nevell Carter into our circle and jeopardized our entire operation. Not to mention that mutha fucka took *beaucoup* money out of my pocket." His tone dripped venom, the betrayal too deep, too costly. "I can never trust you again."

The weight of his words struck like a blow. The air between them was thick, suffocating, filled with the kind of silence that signaled the end.

"I admit bringing Nevell in was a bad idea," Devona pleaded. He looked so promising at the time. It was already too late when I found out he knew Spencer Walach."

A swirl of emotions threatened to consume Devona as her mind slipped away from the present. In a rush of memory, she was back inside *Nevell's study*—the early morning air still thick with tension.

Her fingers trembled over the keyboard as she hacked into Nevell's computer, the glow of the screen casting sharp shadows across her face. Lines of text blurred in her panic until a name cut through the haze—*Spencer Walach.* The message was simple but chilling. Walach had requested a meeting with Nevell.

A cold dread crawled up her spine. She slammed the file shut, her breath shallow and uneven. Heart hammering, she dove beneath Nevell's desk just as the door creaked open.

Nevell stepped inside, his sharp gaze scanning the room. Seconds stretched into eternity. Devona remained perfectly still, forcing down the urge to gulp in air.

Then, as quickly as he had entered, Nevell backed out and shut the door behind him.

The memory faded, slipping like water through her grasp, and she was yanked back to reality—to Trevor's piercing gaze, to the heavy silence between them. Hades continued to grip her wrist, his saliva dripping to pool on the floor.

"You aren't really going to throw me away for *one* mistake," she whispered, voice raw with desperation.

But Trevor's expression remained stone, unmoved.

Trevor stood firm, his eyes sharp with unyielding conviction. His voice was cold, clipped. "In this case, size matters. Big mistake! Huge! "

Devona felt the words land like a slap, but she refused to back down. Her gaze flickered toward Hades, whose dark eyes never wavered from her. He was a statue of controlled power, his presence a silent threat.

She swallowed hard, straightened her posture. "Well, if you're going to leave me here and dissolve the partnership," she said, forcing steel into her voice, "at least let's work out the arrangements for how I'm going to get my share—the one you promised me."

Trevor let out a low, humorless chuckle, shaking his head as he stepped forward. The air between them shrank, thick with something final. "Where you're going," he murmured, his tone dripping with ominous certainty, "you won't need money."

The room felt colder, heavier. Devona realized, perhaps too late, that Trevor wasn't speaking in metaphors—this wasn't just about severing ties. It was about making sure there was *nothing* left to sever.

Devona's sobs came in broken gasps, her body trembling with desperation. "Baby, please! Please don't do this! You don't have to—"

Trevor reached for the door, pulling it open with deliberate ease. He paused, glancing back at her one final time before shifting his gaze to Hades.

Devona's breath hitched as she looked at the massive beast. A deep growl vibrated through the air, primal and unforgiving.

Trevor's voice was calm, nonchalant. "Hades. Devour."

The command lingered like a death sentence.

Devona barely had time to scream before Hades lunged. Trevor stepped into the hallway, shutting the door behind him.

The echoes of her cries faded into the air as Hades tore out Devona's throat.

CHAPTER 75

The park was nearly empty, save for a few lingering shadows stretched long under the golden haze of the setting sun. Simetra sat beside Cecil on the worn wooden bench, the hush of the evening settling over them like a gentle veil. The occasional chirp of a distant bird or the rustling of leaves in the breeze punctuated the silence, but neither of them spoke.

She tightened her grip around her phone, hesitating for a moment before finally dialing. The line rang—once, twice, four, five times—before a voice cut through the quiet.

"I wasn't expecting to hear from you, Ms. Thomas," Levi Stone said smoothly, his voice carrying a warmth laced with curiosity. "But I'm so glad you called. Where are you? I'd be more than happy to come and get you."

Simetra exhaled slowly, watching the dim glow of streetlights flicker on in the distance. A part of her wished things were that simple, that she could let someone else take control just for a moment. But she knew better.

"I can't let you do that, Detective Stone."

A pause on the other end. The silence between them stretched, heavy with unspoken truths.

Cecil shifted beside her, glancing her way, but saying nothing.

Simetra waited for Levi's response, bracing herself for whatever came next.

Simetra sat rigid beside Cecil, her fingers clenched around her phone. The night air was crisp,

A pause. Then Levi spoke again, but this time, his words landed like a gut punch.

"Ms. Thomas, you're wanted for the murder of your brother. You're a fugitive of justice. The Feds are after you. Let me bring you in. It'll make things easier for us both."

Simetra's grip tightened around the phone. "I didn't kill my brother."

Levi exhaled sharply. "Ms. Thomas, my job isn't to accuse you of a crime. It's to ensure you're punished if you commit one. Time is running out. Let me help you before it gets worse.”

Her breath hitched—anger, grief, defiance all tangling into one.

“I know who killed Nevell,” she said, voice steady despite the storm raging inside her. “But I can’t prove it. And since you’re hell-bent on pinning his murder on me, if I come in right now, you’ll let the real killer go free.”

Silence crackled over the line.

“I’m sorry I bothered you,” she murmured, each word carved from stone. “I’m going to have to do this on my own.”

Before he could respond, she ended the call.

Without hesitation, she hurled the phone into the nearby fountain. It hit the water with a splash, sinking beneath the surface, taking with it whatever shred of normalcy she had left.

Beside her, Cecil remained quiet.

The streetlights flickered on. The city hummed around them.

And Simetra knew—there was no turning back now.

At the police department, Levi gripped his phone tightly, jaw clenched as he watched the agent work.

Fingers flew over the keyboard, tracing lines of code, filtering through possibilities. Every second felt like an eternity.

"Did you get anything?" Levi asked, his voice sharp, expectant.

The agent exhaled, shaking his head. "I'm sorry, Detective Stone. We didn't have enough time. It was most likely a burner."

The words landed like a blow.

Levi slammed his fist onto the desk. The sound echoed in the room, but it did nothing to shake the frustration boiling inside him.

Simetra was slipping through his fingers.

Again.

Levi's mind raced, dissecting every word Simetra had said. *I know who killed Nevell.*

What did she mean? Was she grasping at straws, or did she truly have something concrete?

He didn't want to believe she was guilty—
not yet. The evidence was damning, the case
against her airtight. But something nagged at
him, a quiet voice that refused to be ignored.
His gut told him she hadn't killed Nevell.

And if that was true, someone else had.

His grip tightened around the phone, his jaw
clenching as the weight of it all settled. If
she knew even a sliver of truth, she was in
more danger than she realized. He should
bring her in—not just to interrogate her, but
to keep her safe.

If he didn't, she'd be out there alone,
chasing ghosts and putting herself in the
crosshairs of a killer who wouldn't hesitate
to silence her for good.

CHAPTER 76

Nightlife outside the motel is buzzing with traffic.

The room was a scale-up from the Ho Stroll, but not by much.

Cecil set up the computer, fingers moving with practiced ease as he connected the hard drive and booted up the system. The motel room was dim, the neon glow from the street casting shifting colors onto the walls.

He exhaled, settling into the chair. This time, he'd come out like a fat rat—new laptop, fresh burner phone, everything he needed to stay ahead of the game.

At least for now.

Simetra rummaged through her bag for snacks.

Cecil's fingers moved swiftly over the keyboard, the system unlocking layer by layer as he worked. The hum of the motel's old air conditioning unit filled the silence between them.

"Stone didn't believe a word you said," Cecil muttered, his eyes never leaving the screen. "You need to be more careful than ever. He's not just any detective—he's a hard-ass on a mission."

Simetra crossed her arms, staring at the screen. The weight of it all settled heavily on her shoulders.

Cecil exhaled sharply. "I thought we'd be up against the FBI's finest, but Stone…" He shook his head, jaw tightening. "He confirmed my worst fears."

Simetra didn't have to ask what he meant. She already knew.

Stone wasn't just hunting her. It was personal.

He was coming for blood.

The glow of the monitor cast a sharp blue light across the dimly lit motel room. Cecil hunched over the keyboard, fingers flying as lines of code scrolled across the screen. The hard drive whirred softly, processing his every command.

Within minutes, the security feed flickered to life.

On the first screen, a grainy image of Apex Biotech's perimeter came into view—fences, security posts, cameras sweeping methodically. No obvious weaknesses.

Cecil opened another feed. Inside the production plant, workers sat around long tables, assembling intricate components with practiced ease. Laughter echoed through the space, casual and unguarded.

Simetra leaned in, studying the screen, her brow furrowed. *This is going to be harder than I thought.*

Cecil shot her a glance. "Come on, Mama, we've only got a small window that I'm working with."

Another screen opened—a view of the back loading docks. Delivery trucks lined up in neat rows, workers loading crates into the vehicles with swift efficiency.

Simetra's stomach tightened.

Whatever they were looking for—it was here.

And time was slipping through their fingers.

Simetra leaned over Cecil's shoulder. "Rewind the last piece of footage," demanded Simetra, her voice edgy.

Cecil's fingers hovered over the keyboard for a split second before executing the command. The footage rewound, frames flickering backward until the delivery truck reappeared, rolling into the loading dock.

Simetra leaned closer to the screen, scanning every detail.

"You can't be serious about getting inside this place, Mama," Cecil muttered, his voice tight with worry.

She didn't look at him. Her mind was already locked on what had to be done.

"I've got to, Cecil." The words came out firm, unwavering. "Spencer sent Nevell a list—medical supplies that were recalled, damaged, and still used on patients." She inhaled sharply, willing herself to stay focused. "I need hard evidence that they still exist. That's the only way I'm going to prove that one—or both—of those psychopathic twins had a motive to kill Spencer and Nevell."

Cecil exhaled, rubbing his temples. "This is a bad idea."

Simetra straightened, eyes locked on the monitor.

"Maybe," she admitted. "But it's the only one I've got."

Cecil's fingers danced across the keyboard, pulling up schematics, security layouts, anything that could give them an edge.

"I'm checking all the entrances and exits," he muttered, eyes locked on the screen. The glow reflected off his glasses, casting sharp lines across his face. "It's going to be nearly impossible to get inside that building."

Simetra's gaze flickered to the monitor, then back to Cecil.

"Don't worry," she said, a slow grin pulling at the corner of her mouth. "I've got an idea."

CHAPTER 77

The Midtown Medical Supply truck rolled into the dimly lit gas station, the low hum of the engine blending with the distant wail of a siren somewhere across the city. Fluorescent lights flickered overhead, casting a pale glow onto the cracked pavement as the truck eased up beside the pump.

With a grunt, the driver killed the engine and climbed out. He barely glanced at the pump. His mind was already set on cigarettes. The glass doors of the convenience store hissed open, swallowing him into the neon interior.

From the shadows, two figures emerged.

Cecil moved fast, his eyes scanning the lot for any sign of witnesses. Simetra was right behind him, her hoodie drawn low, jaw clenched. In one silent, practiced motion, they unlatched the rear door of the truck. The hinges groaned softly as it opened.

"Go," Cecil whispered.

Simetra didn't hesitate. She climbed inside, slipping into the shadows of cardboard boxes and shrink-wrapped crates.

Cecil hesitated, then pulled the door shut behind her. A quiet *click* echoed as he turned the lock.

Inside the store, the driver wandered the aisles, oblivious. He grabbed a bottle of water, then tossed a pack of mints onto the counter. The cashier looked up when he noticed a motion behind him at the cigarettes.

Outside at the pump, Cecil waves at Simetra before closing the door to the truck, locking her inside.

A minute later, the driver reappeared, stepping back into the night. He cracked open the bottle, took a long sip, and flicked his cigarette pack against his palm. He filled the tank before climbing into the cab. He fired up the engine again, none the wiser.

The truck pulled away from the pump and into the darkness.

Cecil stood watching with a dark sense of foreboding.

The truck rumbled to a halt at the loading dock of Apex Biotech, its arrival unnoticed amidst the quiet hum of late-shift operations. Sodium lights buzzed overhead, casting halos on the rain-slick concrete.

Two warehouse workers rolled up the back door. Pallets waited. Paperwork would follow. None of them looked inside.

Simetra crouched low behind a stack of crates, heart steady, breaths measured. Through the narrow slit of vision between cardboard and steel, she scanned the loading bay. No cameras angled her way. No curious eyes lingered.

With the grace and stealth of a cat, she slipped out of the truck.

Each step echoed faintly as she hugged the wall, glancing once toward a security camera above the office door. It was facing the wrong direction. Perfect.

A left turn. Past the emergency exit. Third door on the right.

The locker room smelled faintly of antiseptic and old coffee. Rows of hooks, a line of steel lockers, and a stack of folded uniforms in a bin labeled *CLEAN*. Simetra moved quickly, pulling a pair of coveralls over her black clothing. A disposable head cover went on last.

She caught her reflection in the mirror above the industrial sink. The disguise wasn't perfect. But with the fluorescent lighting and her confident stride, it would do.

And every step now would matter.

Simetra stumbled around lost until she came to the part of the warehouse where the supplies were being stored on shelves.

She was grateful that the plant was fully automated and didn't have many staff on duty.

The production floor buzzed with a quiet intensity. The conveyor belts whispered. Machines hissed and clicked in rhythm. Under harsh industrial lighting, a single masked worker moved methodically, sealing, sorting, and scanning.

Simetra slipped onto the floor like she belonged.

Her mask hugged the lower half of her face, concealing more than just her expression. She kept her eyes down, her movements mimicking the repetitive tasks around her.

The worker never looked up. He seemed not to care.

She could have been anyone.

A clipboard-wielding supervisor appeared, passing close to Simetra. He nodded absently as he scribbled something unreadable. Simetra turned away, just slightly hoping not to be noticed. Just another cog in the machine.

It worked.

Minutes later, she peeled away from the line and exited through a side door marked **WAREHOUSE.**

The instant she stepped into the cavernous space, the sound changed.

A roar of motion surrounded her—robotic arms loading pallets with surgical precision, forklifts navigating like chess pieces across the gleaming floor. Overhead, drone-like lifters zipped from shelf to shelf, stacking crates almost forty feet high. The air was laced with the sterile scent of chemicals and cardboard.

Simetra kept walking.

She moved deeper into the open space. Her gaze flitted from one aisle marker to the next, tracing the digital signs that blinked their inventory stats. Then, she saw it.

Halfway down the southern wall—nestled between two towers of insulated crates—a narrow lift shaft, its polished door barely wider than her shoulders. It looked like a dumbwaiter, though far too sleek to be antiquated.

She paused, ahead of her, a worker scanned barcodes on a nearby crate. The lift might be the key. Or a dead end.

Either way, it was the next move.

The hum of the lift echoed as it slid up and down the shaft, dispatching sterile packages to unseen levels of the warehouse. Simetra watched it for a moment, timing its rhythm. Silently, she gauged how long she'd have before it returned.

Then she moved on.

Beyond a row of stacked crates, she stumbled upon a quiet alcove. Four electric carts were parked neatly in a bay marked *INTERNAL TRANSPORT ONLY.*

Simetra approached the nearest cart. Its digital display blinked to life when she tapped the console. The key was still in the ignition.

She slipped into the seat.

The cart purred as it started, gliding forward like a whisper on wheels. Ahead, a piercing white light broke through a narrow corridor that ran along the back wall of the warehouse. It wasn't part of the standard industrial glow—this light was contained, focused, like a signal or… an invitation.

She followed it.

The cart's tires squeaked on the polished concrete as she slowed near the wall's edge. There, tucked in a recessed corner like a forgotten secret, was a steel-framed office. Its door was ajar.

Soft light spilled out, catching motes of dust in the air.

Simetra stepped down silently, leaving the cart idling behind her. She crept to the doorway.

Inside, a man sat at a desk, leaning back in an ergonomic chair with one leg casually draped over the other. He wore a tailored vest over his button-down shirt, sleeves rolled to the elbow. A biometric tablet flickered on the desk in front of him, but his eyes were fixed on her.

He looked as if he'd been expecting someone.

"Simetra," he said, with a calm that didn't match the flicker of coldness in his eyes. "You made better time than I thought."

Trevor Knox.

CHAPTER 78

The electric cart gave a soft whir as Simetra stepped off. Her boots clicked softly against the polished concrete, each step measured, precise.

Trevor Knox sat behind the desk like he owned the building—and maybe he did. His long legs were crossed casually, one arm resting across the chair back, the other holding a bright red bullhorn like it was an afterthought. The corner of his mouth quirked with amusement as he looked up from the desk.

"So nice of you to drop in, Ms. Thomas," he said, his voice slow and self-satisfied. "I've been expecting you."

Simetra remained in the doorway, her eyes sharp, unblinking. "Are you Scott or Trevor?"

Trevor leaned forward, setting the bullhorn down with a quiet *clack*. His eyes gleamed with something unreadable—humor, maybe. Or danger.

"Trust your gut, Ms. Thomas," he said. "I think you know who I am."

She studied him in silence. The cadence of his voice, the smile that never quite reached his eyes. Something about it felt familiar.

"You have to be Trevor," she said at last, her tone cool. "Although… I feel like you're Scott."

For a heartbeat, something flickered behind his gaze. Then it was gone.

"You'd be surprised how often people confuse the two of us," he said smoothly. "The truth depends on what you came here looking for."

Simetra took a single step into the office, letting the door fall quietly shut behind her. The silence that followed was heavy, intimate.

Trevor still lounged behind the desk, bullhorn discarded beside a holographic tablet. His expression was unreadable, but his eyes tracked her every move with quiet calculation.

"I would have never made the connection that you were twins without seeing you," she said, watching for a reaction.

Trevor smiled faintly. "Knox is my mother's maiden name. I was born Colton, but changed my name when I left for college. Wanted to sever ties. Create distance." He shrugged, eyes drifting briefly toward the wall-mounted security panel. "Eventually, I learned to appreciate the curse of having a sibling with the exact same face."

Simetra's gaze swept the room—a neat rectangle of frosted glass and reinforced steel. One way in. One way out. Her jaw tightened.

"The two of you sharing everything must be rewarding," she said, her tone carefully neutral.

Trevor's eyes sharpened. "My brother is my other half," he replied, leaning forward just enough to make her feel it. "It took me longer than most to realize he's the only person I could truly trust."

He paused, then added, "Unfortunately, he doesn't trust anyone. Least of all you."

That last line lingered in the air like smoke, and for the first time, something shifted in Simetra's expression. Not fear. Not guilt. Just… quiet acknowledgment.

Trevor raised a brow, his mouth curling into a half-smile. "He told me all about you."

Simetra folded her arms, gaze steady. "All bad, I'm sure. But I don't care," she added, not waiting for confirmation. "I came here to put an end to you and your brother's little game of Russian Roulette with other people's lives."

Trevor's smile didn't falter, but something in his eyes cooled. He leaned back in his chair, fingers tapping a slow rhythm against the armrest.

"And how do you plan to do that?"

A beat.

Then, as if remembering something amusing, he straightened, reached down behind the desk, and pulled out a sleek, jet-black case. With a dramatic click, he opened it.

"Oh yes," he said smoothly, lifting the lid to reveal a row of sleek ID badges, digital key fobs, and a small metallic vial tucked into padded lining. "You must be looking for at least one of these."

Simetra's eyes narrowed.

"Take your pick," Trevor said. "Each one opens a door to a different kind of truth."

He leaned forward, elbows on the desk now. "But be careful which one you choose, Ms. Thomas. Some doors don't close again."

Simetra's gaze drifted to the box beside the desk. A handful of medical supplies stuck out from the top: blister packs of injectables, neatly labeled vials, and a slender diagnostics wand wrapped in a hospital-blue seal.

She stepped closer.

"These are…" she began, her voice faltering as recognition set in.

Trevor cut her off smoothly, his tone almost indulgent. "You guessed it."

He stood, moving around the desk with unhurried confidence, the box now between them like a shared secret.

"These are some of the original prototypes Spencer Walach flagged," he said. "Faulty, according to him. A bit melodramatic, if you ask me. But Spencer—he had this thing about integrity."

Trevor glanced at Simetra, reading her silence.

"That was always his weakness," he added. "He was too smart for his own good. Dug too deep. Talked too much. You can imagine my dilemma when I found out he was warning our investors behind my back."

Simetra's jaw tightened. Her fingers hovered just over one of the vials.

"You silenced him," she said quietly.

Trevor didn't answer. He didn't need to.

Simetra already knew the answer. They had done something horrific to Spencer. That's why he was living on the streets.

Trevor Knox reached into the open box and pulled out a sleek, palm-sized device—its brushed metal casing gleaming under the office's sterile lights.

A portable breathing machine.

He cradled it like a prized artifact, holding it aloft for Simetra to see. "I'm sure you'd love to get your hands on this little baby right here," he said, his voice dipped in mock generosity.

Then, without warning, he stepped forward and extended it to her.

"Go ahead," he murmured. "Take it."

Simetra hesitated. Her instincts screamed caution, but her mission whispered urgency. She reached out and wrapped her fingers around the machine.

Trevor's hand didn't let go.

Instead, he grasped her forearm, holding it just tightly enough to register the pressure. His smile didn't budge. His eyes didn't blink. Then, slowly, he released her arm, letting the machine transfer fully into her hands.

Simetra's pulse thrummed. She stared at him, the device cool against her skin.

"What's the catch?" she asked, her voice razor-thin.

Trevor took a measured step back, his tone calm and almost amused. "Therein, my dear Ms. Thomas," he said, folding his arms, "lies your dilemma. How are you going to get out of here with it?"

Simetra clutched the breathing device tight against her chest, cradling it like a football as she burst through the office door. Her boots thundered across the polished concrete, every stride echoing through the warehouse like a starter pistol.

She dove onto the golf cart, yanked the key, and floored it.

The engine whirred to life, sending the cart lurching forward just as Trevor stepped calmly into the doorway behind her, unhurried, composed, the bullhorn dangling from his hand.

He turned, eyes tracking her as the vehicle zipped away, then walked to a low cage built into the wall. A metal grate door. No labels.

Simetra hadn't noticed it. No one would have.

Trevor crouched, unlatched the door, and reached in with one hand. "Hades," he said softly, offering his fingers to the pit bull curled in the shadows. The dog had been silent the entire time. He dog sniffed Trevor's hand, catching Simetra's scent. His tail still, eyes alert.

"Hades… search."

The pit bull stepped out with almost regal composure, muscles rippling beneath its coat, gaze locked onto the scent that was different from its master's.

Simetra took a sharp turn down one of the corridors, heart pounding. She glanced over her shoulder once, just in time to see Trevor in the distance, standing calm as ever, watching as his predator slipped into the shadows in pursuit.

And Hades… didn't bark.

He ran like a sprinter towards the finish line.

The golf cart skidded as Simetra rounded the curve too sharply, the tires squealing in protest before the entire frame tipped sideways. In a blur of motion, the cart flipped.

She hit the ground hard, rolling across the concrete, the breath knocked from her lungs.

But she didn't stop.

Clutching the breathing device tight to her chest, she scrambled to her feet and broke into a run, darting between towers of boxed medical equipment that loomed like city blocks. The warehouse was a maze, and she didn't know the layout—but it didn't matter. All that mattered was staying ahead of Hades.

And he was certainly coming.

At the end of one aisle, a low sound—barely more than breath on wind.

Hades.

The pit bull moved with eerie precision, muscles rippling under brindled fur, its nose lowered to the concrete. At the end of each row, it paused, lifted its head, and sniffed the air. Calculating. Homing in.

Simetra flattened herself behind a stack of diagnostic equipment. She could hear the dog's footsteps—unhurried, confident. Twice, it passed within feet of her hiding spot. Once, it stopped altogether, head tilted as if listening to the silence itself.

Then it moved on.

Above it all, a voice rang out from the warehouse's speaker system, bouncing off steel and shadow.

"Olly Olly Oxen Free…" Trevor's voice sang, saccharine and cold.

"Ms. Thomas," he drawled through the bullhorn, "you can't hide from me."

Simetra's jaw clenched. Her pulse thundered in her ears.

She didn't need to hide forever.

Just long enough to turn the game around.

CHAPTER 79

Simetra sprinted through the maze of towering crates, her pulse screaming in her ears. The breathing device clutched to her chest weighed more with each stride, like it was absorbing her fear. Hades was close. She could feel the heat of his breath behind her, hear the clicking of claws against concrete.

Then—the lift.

A narrow silver panel flush with the wall. Her only shot.

She lunged toward it, knocking over a trio of compact sorting bots in the process. The little machines spun and clattered, their blinking sensors swiveling in confusion. Simetra slammed her palm onto the glowing *UP* button. The doors parted just wide enough for her to dive inside.

She turned.

Hades was already mid-sprint, a silent force of muscle and instinct.

The lift doors slid shut just as the pit bull leapt.

A heavy *thud* shook the metal.

Simetra collapsed back against the wall, her chest heaving, the device still cradled protectively. The elevator jerked and began its ascent. Through the narrowing gap of the closing doors, she caught one last glimpse of Hades, sitting perfectly still at the base of the lift, head tilted, watching her rise. Patient. Unblinking.

The doors sealed with a mechanical sigh.

Moments later, the lift opened onto a narrow catwalk suspended high above the warehouse. Rows of products stretched endlessly in every direction beneath her— crates, drones, motion, and metal. Simetra stepped off, the walkway creaking underfoot.

No one up here.

But Trevor wouldn't wait long to change that.

The lift doors closed behind her with a soft *chime*, descending again into the shadows below. Simetra stood alone on the elevated walkway, the hush of the warehouse pressing in like static. Her breath slowed, but her muscles stayed coiled, ready.

She stepped lightly across the catwalk,
scanning every junction, every possible exit.

Then came the growl.

Low. Rumbling. Ancient.

She froze.

Rounding the next corner, Simetra stopped
cold. A massive Rottweiler stood at the edge
of the platform—its black-and-mahogany
coat gleaming under the overhead lights, its
head lowered, eyes locked onto her.

Two words split the silence.

"Calli, hold!" Trevor's voice called up,
distorted faintly by distance. From
somewhere unseen below, his bullhorn
echoed with eerie calm.

But the command came a heartbeat too late.

With predatory precision, the dog lunged—
not to bite, but to clamp her blouse in its
iron jaws. Simetra staggered backward, too
shocked to scream, her limbs locked with
terror as the fabric bunched and pulled
across her shoulder.

She couldn't breathe.

Her grip slipped. The portable breathing machine tumbled from her hands and struck the metal grate with a hollow *clang*, skittering toward the edge like it might fall into oblivion.

Simetra didn't move.

She could feel the dog's breath through the fabric. A low warning hum rattled in Calli's throat, vibrating against her ribs.

Below, Trevor chuckled softly into the bullhorn.

"Did you think I wouldn't plan for altitude?"

Trevor's voice echoed through the metal expanse, amplified by the bullhorn with calm authority. "They only attack on my command."

Simetra didn't move. Her breath came shallow and rapid, eyes locked on the Rottweiler's massive jaw, clenched around her blouse. Every muscle in her body screamed to run, but instinct knew better.

A mechanical chime sounded behind her.

The lift.

Trevor Knox ascended slowly, arms folded behind his back like he was rising to greet royalty. As the doors opened, he stepped out without hesitation, the bullhorn now dangling casually at his side.

He knelt beside the dog.

"Calli," he said, voice smooth. "Release."

The Rottweiler let go of Simetra's blouse. The tension broke with a moist snap of fabric. Calli gave Simetra a single, deliberate sniff—then let out a low, throaty growl that vibrated in her bones.

Trevor stroked the dog's head affectionately.

"Calli… rest."

The beast sat obediently, her haunches lowering like a queen taking her throne. But her eyes never left Simetra.

Trevor stood and turned to face her, his steps unhurried. He closed the distance in silence.

Then—*crack.*

The back of his hand caught her across the cheek in a whip-fast blur, sending her stumbling dangerously toward the edge. Her foot caught the metal grate. Her shoulder slammed into the safety rail.

She nearly went over.

But Simetra's instincts kicked in. Her fingers latched onto the cold metal bar, hooking her arm through just in time to stop the fall. Her knees scraped hard against steel. The breathing machine skittered out of reach, spinning near the platform's edge.

Trevor towered over her.

"I always said," he murmured, too softly for the bullhorn, "that trust is earned. And you're still very much overdrawn."

"Ms. Thomas," Trevor drawled, brushing imaginary dust from his sleeve, "you're no fun at all. You made this too easy."

Simetra stood her ground, blood seeping from the corner of her mouth, the sting still fresh from his backhand.

"You know," he added, casually lifting his hand for another strike, "I can't let you leave here alive."

Trevor threw a punch, but the blow never landed.

Simetra's arm shot up, blocking the hit with a sharp crack of bone against bone. In the same instant, she pivoted and slammed her knee into his groin.

Trevor crumpled with a grunt, doubling over in disbelief. His breath hitched in his throat as he dropped to one knee.

Simetra backed away, wiping the blood from her lip with the back of her hand.

Trevor rose slowly, rage twisting his features. "You have no idea who you're messing with."

"Trust me, Ditto," Simetra spat, her voice low and deadly.

He lunged.

She met him in the air.

Her foot connected cleanly with his jaw—an explosion of pain and momentum. Trevor went airborne, crashing into a stack of boxes with a thunderous *crash*. Crates toppled around him. A metal tray clattered to the floor, followed by a wet cough as he spat out blood.

Simetra squared her shoulders, chest heaving. The breathing device still lay at the edge of the platform, just beyond reach.

But she wasn't finished yet.

Trevor staggered upright, blood streaking his chin, pride more injured than flesh. His eyes darted toward Callie, still seated and waiting, every muscle ready for the next command.

"I've had enough of this," he snarled. "Callie—"

Simetra thought fast and moved even faster.

Her boot cracked across his mouth mid-syllable, silencing the word before it reached the air. Trevor's head snapped back. His body lifted from the ground and sailed over the railing.

His scream echoed throughout the warehouse.

The sound he made as he struck the concrete below was something far worse—a sickening, final *thud*.

Trevor Knox lay twisted and still, limbs crooked at unnatural angles. Hades stood at his side and whined softly, confused, ears flat against his skull.

Above, Simetra leaned on the railing, chest rising in heavy bursts. Blood streaked her jawline. The breathing machine sat untouched by her feet. Beside her, Callie whimpered, her posture still rigid. The command half-given had left her in limbo.

Simetra turned to the dog.

"It's a good thing," she whispered, voice ragged, "you can only attack on his command."

Callie blinked, but didn't move.

For the first time that night, Simetra allowed herself to hope the silence meant it was over.

Simetra leaned against the catwalk railing, her knuckles raw and streaked with dust and blood. Callie remained motionless beside her, the Rottweiler's wide eyes blinking slowly, processing a world that had just shifted beneath its paws.

She pulled out her phone with fingers that barely stopped shaking and hit the speed dial.

One ring.

Two.

"Mama?" Cecil's voice crackled through the speaker, thick with worry. "Are you alright?"

Simetra stared at the wreckage below, where the body of Trevor Knox lay twisted in eternal stillness.

"I will be," she said quietly.

A pause, then, "What about Knox?"

She exhaled hard, wiping her mouth with the back of her hand. "He's in no position to hurt anyone ever again."

Another beat.

"I'm on my way."

She glanced down the catwalk, already hearing the distant hum of systems coming back online—recovery teams wouldn't be far behind.

"Come and get me," she said. "And make it fast."

CHAPTER 80

Morning light cut through the blinds like a scalpel, sharp and sterile. Scott Colton sat motionless behind his desk, eyes fixed on the soft glow of his monitor. His fingertips pressed into his chest—slow, firm pressure where the discomfort had bloomed.

He reached for the glass of water beside the keyboard, took a shallow sip, and let the sensation pass. Not gone, just... postponed.

The call icon blinked softly on his screen.

He tapped it.

Silence.

Then a robotic voice filtered through the speaker: *"The number you have dialed is unavailable. Please try again later."*

Scott frowned.

He tried again.

Same message.

His jaw tightened.

"I haven't heard from you this morning," he muttered into the phone, voice laced with irritation and just the faintest thread of anxiety. "Call me when you get a chance."

He ended the call without waiting for a response and turned back to his desktop. With a few keystrokes, he pulled up the building's surveillance interface—camera logs arranged like tiles. One caught his eye: *Exterior - Electroshock Treatment Room - 03:17 A.M.*

He clicked it.

The footage flickered to life, shadows dancing across the screen. The silence in the office thickened, like the calm before something broke.

Scott leaned in, eyes narrowing.

He had a feeling he wouldn't like what he was about to see.

Scott sat in the half-light of his office, fingertips tapping the keyboard with surgical precision. The video bloomed to life on his monitor: grainy surveillance footage with a timestamp blinking in the lower corner, right at shift change when the unit would be empty. The nurses would be exchanging notes on patients' charts and going over treatment plans.

Carla had gone against protocol and applied Walach's treatment after her shift. Lucky for Scott, she had been so careless and so naive.

On-screen, Carla Benyon stepped into the hallway, peering cautiously down both directions before slipping back inside the treatment room.

Scott's figure slid into frame behind her. Quiet. Invisible.

A few seconds later, Justin Ambrose entered the room. The two spoke briefly—no audio, just shapes in the dim light. Carla turned toward the console and flipped the electroshock machine's activation switch.

Nothing happened.

Behind her, Scott stepped forward and leveled a Taser at Justin. One jolt—and the young man crumpled to the floor, twitching violently.

Carla spun, only to be met with the same electric fate. Her scream tore through the soundtrack, distorted and metallic. It lasted longer than it should have.

Then Scott—the Scott watching the recording—saw himself on-screen walk to the console and calmly flip the switch.

Spencer Walach's body jolted upright on the table, limbs snapping in grotesque rhythm. The machine sparked faintly as Spencer convulsed, his muscles pulling tight like marionette strings. Scott, on-screen, watched with chilling satisfaction, arms crossed like a man admiring his own reflection.

The footage ended in silence.

Scott blinked once.

Then he deleted the file.

No hesitation.

No second glance.

For weeks, Carla and Justin had carried the weight in silence. Scott's lie had been neat, cruel, and convincing: a sudden EMP, an unexplained blackout, both of them unconscious. Spencer Walach—so he told them—had been electrocuted in the chaos. A tragic accident, nothing more.

They'd believed it. At first.

And when suspicion crept in—when the cracks in Scott's version grew too wide to ignore—he was waiting with veiled threats and cold reminders of their employment contracts.

"Talk," he'd said, "and neither of you works again."

But in the end, silence wasn't enough.

He fired them anyway. Swept them out like debris from a crime scene.

Lucky for him, all of his loose ends had been tied up like a bow. By deleting the video, there was nothing left to tie him to any crime.

Scott Colton barely looked up from his computer screen as the door to his office opened. "What is it now, Detective Stone?" he muttered, his voice soaked in disdain. "Can't we stop playing this game? Somebody clearly doesn't have enough true crimes to keep themselves entertained."

Detective Levi Stone stepped inside, calm and direct. He didn't bother closing the door behind him.

"On the contrary," Levi said, slipping a folded sheet of paper from his jacket pocket, "I'm solving a very real one. Right now."

Scott's smirk wavered.

"You can't charge me with anything," he snapped.

Levi held the warrant between two fingers and let it unfurl. "This says I can. And I will."

Then, as if unveiling a trump card, he pulled a thumb drive from his coat and held it out like an executioner's blade.

"The files you just deleted?" Levi said evenly. "They're backed up right here. This little bad boy has all of your dirty deeds recorded. I've been watching you longer than you think."

The blood drained from Scott's face.

"Scott Colton," Levi said, stepping forward, "you're under arrest."

Scott stiffened. For a moment, he looked like he might argue—might fight. But instead, he slowly turned and placed his hands behind his back, deflated.

The cold click of handcuffs sealed the silence between them.

Levi leaned close, his voice like ice. "By the way… Trevor Knox is dead."

Scott inhaled sharply. His chest buckled. His knees threatened to give. Pain—or rage—twisted his features.

Levi didn't wait.

He shoved him forward, out the door, and into the light.

CHAPTER 81

The sun cast long, golden rays across the training grounds of the Government Canine Center. Callie trotted through an obstacle course, her movements deliberate, guided by calm commands. A trainer knelt and offered a steady hand. She responded with a gentle nudge and a trusting gaze.

Nearby, Hades walked beside a soldier in a wheelchair, matching pace, alert but calm. The former hunter now wore a vest that read: *Emotional Support – Do Not Distract.* His eyes were softer now, purpose reshaped.

The past was behind them. Their future was one of healing.

Dust rose in spirals from the Mercy Hospital construction site as bulldozers carved new edges into the earth. Workers in neon vests directed the dance of cranes and concrete mixers. Rebar caught the light like bones of a structure not yet born.

At the edge of the chaos, a new sign gleamed:

COMING SOON – **The Carter Center for Brain Injury Research**

Simetra stood alone in the shadow of its promise.

Her voice came softly, carried on memory.

"It's so hard not having you around to give me hell. But no worries—I'm going to be alright."

She looked up, letting the breeze tug at her collar.

"Mercy is breaking ground. They're building a place where pain might actually end. Where questions get answered. So rest easy, Bubba... until I see you again."

She walked forward, hand brushing the edge of the sign as the wind swirled dust into the air, like old ghosts being swept into light.

Cecil leaned against the passenger door, hands tucked in the pockets of a navy-blue suit that had definitely seen better days—but on him, it looked like purpose. His tie was slightly crooked. His smile, perfectly steady.

"I decided to do Old Spence proud," he said, meeting her eyes. "Try to get my life back. They're giving me a second chance at Quantico."

Simetra's face lit up, the pride in her expression unmistakable. "That's what I'm talking about," she said, stepping in for a hug. "I'm happy for you."

Then, with the kind of smirk only she could deliver, she added, "You're gonna need that job."

Cecil raised a brow. "Why's that?"

"Because you owe me back rent."

He laughed, that same boyish laugh that hadn't surfaced in months, maybe longer. She hadn't realized how much she missed it.

They stood there a moment longer as construction rumbled in the distance, the future being built brick by stubborn brick.

The End

Artemis Craig

Bio

Artemis is an author, poet, and screenwriter.

She grew up the fourth of nine children. Her parents, a coal miner/steelworker father and an educator mother, were instrumental in developing her love for writing. She graduated from the University of Southern California film school with a B.F.A.

Artemis co-wrote the screenplay for the movie *"Plus Size"*, with Men in the Kingdom Productions, where she tried her hand at acting and directing. She also had a role in the movie *"Acting Out."*

Her collection of poems, *"Inspirational Verse for Those Who Hunger and Thirst"* (2013) reflects her Baptist/Pentecostal roots, where she uses lyrical poetry to inspire others to find their inner peace and strength through faith.

After retiring, Artemis devotes her time to writing and reciting poetry at the **Inspired Poetry Corner,** a community of artists who share their truth through spoken word.

She enjoys being out in nature and basking in the love of her family.

Value of Blood: The Price of Truth